The Christmas Clause

Copyright © 2023 by Meg Easton

All rights reserved.

No part of this book may be reproduced in any form or by any electronic or mechanical means, including information storage and retrieval systems, without written permission from the author, except for the use of brief quotations in a book review.

This is a work of fiction and names, characters, incidents, and places are products of the author's imagination or used fictitiously. Any resemblance to persons, living or dead, incidents, and places is coincidental.

Cover Illustration: Alt19 Creative

Interior design: Mountain Heights Publishing

Author website: www.megeaston.com

How to Not Fall for Your Ex

A Mountain Springs Christmas

The Christmas Pact

The Christmas Bet

The Christmas Clause

Love Started Romances

It Started with a Sunset

It Started with a Note

It Started with a Glance

Silver Leaf Falls romance

Coming Home to Silver Leaf Falls

The Christmas Clause

the christmas clause

A SWEET HOLIDAY ROMANCE

MEG EASTON

MOUNTAIN HEIGHTS
— PUBLISHING —

For everyone who needs something a bit unexpected this Christmas

contents

one

KATIE

KATIE PICKED up a sprig of spruce and a few stems of berries and placed them in the centerpiece she was working on. "I want a guy who will serenade me. Even if he can't sing."

"And I want..." her roommate, best friend, and owner of this shop, Emmalee, said as she trimmed a bunch of amaryllis stems, "a guy with a sense of adventure who never gets lost."

Katie turned the centerpiece she was working on around, checking it from all angles. "And, of course, a guy who could come up with the perfect late-night snack at a moment's notice."

Emmalee stopped her trimming to give Katie a flat stare. "Really. You would sit on Santa's lap, look him straight in the eyes, and ask for a man who will make you pizza rolls at midnight."

"I'm sure he's heard more ridiculous requests."

"Okay, then." Emmalee grinned. "I want a guy who's a gourmet chef and specializes in breakfast foods."

It was ironic that Emmalee brought up the subject of qualities they'd like in a man, since it hadn't even been fifteen minutes since she said she was never going to date another man again, ever. Katie, though? She was always down to have fun casual dating. That was, of course, until the right man swept her off her feet.

And she'd made it a goal to stop wanting to date a guy based on first impressions so she could up her chances of finding that man who would do the sweeping. Usually, she found out after a date or two that a guy wasn't quite what she'd thought at first impression. Which wasn't always bad— she'd dated quite a few guys who made for interesting dates but didn't have a chance at being her happily ever after. But now, she was all-in on slowing down and finding out more first.

She just didn't really believe that getting swept off her feet would happen. At least not until she was at least thirty. Six more years wasn't that long to wait, right? Until then, she was going to keep building her videography business and helping Emmalee build her floral business.

It actually worked out well for both of them. This

flower shop was barely big enough for the two of them to work in— any customers who came had to stand outside at the window to place or pick up an order. But it was adorable and was right on Main Street in their small town of Mountain Springs. Emmalee got to do what she loved, and Katie got a part-time job that worked with the crazy schedule she often had as she worked to accommodate her clients' videography needs. Plus, it was fun to work side by side with her friend and roommate.

And okay, sometimes when there were big events, like prom, a wedding, or Valentine's day, the flower shop wasn't big enough, and her roommate's business spilled into their apartment. On the plus side, though, their apartment often smelled great.

And right now, the flower shop smelled pretty incredible. Christmas floral arrangements meant a lot of poinsettias, azaleas, roses, orchids, and pine cones. Combine it with the scent of pine sprigs, and it might just be Katie's favorite scent. Add in the Christmas music playing through a small Bluetooth speaker on the counter and their view of all the Christmas decorations that were currently going up on Main Street, and Katie was ready to dream of a white Christmas, deck the halls (or the living room) of their apartment, rock around their Christmas tree (once they got it put up) and jingle all the way to her Christmas shopping.

As well as Emmalee's business was going, it still had

its feast and famine moments. Sometimes, Emmalee could use all the help that Katie could possibly give, and at other times, there wasn't enough business for Katie to work at all. She definitely couldn't rely on working at the flower shop to cover her expenses.

Not that Katie wanted to ever have to rely on Emmalee's business for the ability to pay her bills. Especially because Katie was really good at videography. It was her passion, and every client raved about the final product. Making customers happy came easy for her. In a small town, though, word of mouth only went to so many people.

Her videography business might still be a fledgling one, but she had big plans for it. And one of those was to make enough in her busier months to not only cover the less busy months but to give her a big, "I've got this" cushion. There was nothing scarier than thinking that maybe she couldn't get all she needed on her own.

Katie sighed. "I've got to find a way to get more business. And not just soon, but on a regular basis."

"Do you have any ideas?"

"That are cheap or free until I can build up an advertising budget? Beyond trying to convince people in Mountain Springs and Nestled Hollow that they'd benefit by having a professional videographer at more events in their lives and posting about my business on social media in neighborhood groups outside of our area, nothing yet. But if I don't find a way to grow my business soon, then I'm going to be living out of my car."

"You're not going to have to live out of your car."

"I'll be living out of my car and eating those cheap packages of Ramen. Which might not work out so well, because I don't exactly have a kitchenette in my car. Oh! Maybe I could get some of those Styrofoam cups of soup that you just add water to. Then maybe I could use a convenience store's microwave or something."

"Don't be silly. Your bedroom is still the same as it was the day you moved out, right? You could just move back in with your parents."

Wait. Was that why they kept it the same instead of turning it into the guest bedroom that they said they were going to? In case her business failed? "I'm not moving back home. That would mean admitting defeat or admitting that I need help."

"And you can do neither. Okay, I'll tell you what. If your business fails and you end up living out of your car, then I will move into my car, too, in solidarity with you. We can park next to each other, open the doors between our cars, and put a big blanket over it. It can be a fort and we can pretend we are just having a sleepover like when we were kids."

"You'd do it out of solidarity? Or because you couldn't pay for rent on your own?"

Emmalee shrugged. "Call it whatever."

Katie was just putting the arrangement she'd finished in the fridge when her phone rang, lighting up the screen with a picture of her dad smiling back at her. She answered and said, "Hi, Dad. You're on speaker phone—Emmalee is here."

She and Emmalee always answered calls they weren't willing to take outside in the cold on speaker phone. If the other person in this small space had to listen to one side of the conversation, it was only polite to let them hear the other half, too. Plus, it kept their hands free for working.

She grabbed a new vase as her dad said, "Hi, Sweetie. Hi, Emmalee. Okay, so you know how I've been working on that project to rebuild the Glaciers' team image?"

Katie nodded. "Especially after all the damage that the Player Who Shall Not Be Named did." For not being a huge fan of professional hockey, Katie knew a good number of random things about Denver's team. Mostly because her dad was in charge of branding for the team. She just didn't know much about most of the players.

"Exactly. Well, my plan to have the players spread out to help out with Christmas festivities in towns all around the state is a go. My team and I have jumped through all the hoops to get it approved and everyone on board, even the players."

"That's great, Dad," Katie said as she tilted her head

at the roses she had just put into the vase, seeing if it looked like enough to create the picture she had in her head.

"I think so, too. And I am calling in an official capacity for the Denver Glaciers to offer a short-term contract to you to be a videographer for one of the players."

"Wait. For real?" The thrill of a job for her very own company with the Denver Glaciers hit at the same time as the deep-in-her-soul resistance she always had to people trying to do things for her that she could do herself. "Dad, I can't take it. I need to build my company by getting jobs because of my own merit, not because I'm your daughter."

"You did get this because of your own merit."

Katie picked up a stem with a few white azalea blooms and dark green leaves but didn't do anything with it. "I'm listening."

"We asked the players to submit names of towns they'd like to do some Christmas outreach with. Then my team and I split the state into areas and I assigned each area to someone on my team. We want videogra- phers local to each area we are sending players— we aren't just doing this for our image, we're also doing it to help out the communities who support us, which includes supporting local videographers.

"Each of my team members scoured the areas assigned to them for the best videographers. Then they brought their list to our meeting and, area by area, we voted on which videographer to ask.

"I knew you wouldn't want me to, so I didn't say a single thing about you. My team found you on their own and had no idea at the time that there was a relation between me and KatieVid. When the portfolios of videographers in our area came up for a vote, they chose you unanimously."

"They chose me? For real? Without knowing who I am?"

"For real."

She might have squealed. Or maybe it was Emmalee. It was probably both of them. "I'll take the job!" She had filmed and edited videos for quite a few sporting events (high school games and little kids' soccer matches) and plenty of Christmas events. Lots of weddings, milestone birthdays, concerts, recitals, performances, and the occasional family reunion.

Never anything like filming a professional hockey player doing town Christmas events, though. To be able to put the Denver Glaciers on her site as one of her clients was *huge*. "When do I start?"

"Likely within the next week or so, depending on the player's schedule— I'll get you the details as soon as I can. A lot of the players are set for different locations, but ours isn't yet. I'll still get you the contract to sign soon, and then we'll get with the mayor and come up with a plan."

After thanking her dad profusely, she hung up the phone.

"This is huge for your business," Emmalee said.

"My website is going to look so great having the Denver Glaciers' logo in my client's section! I might be able to start getting business outside of the Mountain Springs area. I might be able to see some real growth." Katie had set some major goals for her business that she had hoped to accomplish by the end of the year, and she was worried that she wouldn't meet the goals. This would definitely help.

She and Emmalee just grinned at each other. Then Emmalee asked, "Which player do you think you're going to get? Oh, maybe it'll be Bradshaw."

"Which one is he again?" Katie really should memorize the players some time. She didn't need to know them as well as Emmalee did, but her dad had worked for the Glaciers for five years— she should know them by now. She just hadn't really found a love for the sport yet.

"The super hot one with the dark wavy hair. The *recently single* super hot one. I hope it's him. Ooo, maybe it'll be the bad boy, Ackerman. Although, no, your dad would never assign him to you. In fact, if there isn't a player that your dad approves of for his youngest daughter, he'll likely assign a married player to Mountain Springs."

Katie nodded. She was totally fine with that. "Maybe it'll be that one guy with the adorable wife and two little kids. The one that just had a baby."

"Davis? I'm obsessed with him and his cute family. Seriously, relationship goals there. *If* I was going to ever get into a relationship again, which I'm not."

Katie patted her friend on the shoulder. "Of course, you aren't." She totally was. "And my dad said he asked the players where they wanted to go, so I'm sure he'll honor their wishes first."

"True," Emmalee said, tapping a rose against her lips as she pondered, the top thorn getting dangerously close to her chin with each tap. "So it could be anyone. I would assign you homework to learn who all of the players are, but we both know you're not going to do it unless someone makes you. So, as your boss in this shop, for the next two hours that you'll be on duty, I am your teacher. I'm going to give you a rundown of all twenty-one players. By the time we finish today, you'll be able to recognize any of them on sight. Because girl, you need to know who is on your own team."

She really did. As someone who grew up a thirty-minute drive from Denver, the Glaciers were "her team." As Reid Allred's daughter, they were doubly her team. By blood. Plus, she needed to be prepared for whichever player she got assigned, so she nodded. "Let's do this."

two

CONNOR

CONNOR STRODE over to the aisle with shaving razors, a shopping basket on his arm, his phone at his ear, listening to his sister, Laura. She was making her way through his house, gathering things he needed.

"These contact lenses are daily-wear ones, right? I've got you a week's worth and your glasses case." She let out a big exhale and he heard the drawer shut. "I can't believe they didn't let you spend five minutes at home to pack a bag before you left."

Connor scanned the choices of razors. "There was no way I could've driven all the way home from the arena and turned around to immediately drive back to the airport— even without going inside and packing a bag— and still made that flight."

"Where are your glasses?"

"Nightstand."

"And there's really no way for you to come back home for Christmas?

Connor scanned the razors again but didn't see the brand he normally used. Maybe he would just leave the scruff. "I used in-flight WiFi any moment I wasn't fielding messages from TV analysts and reps from the Glaciers to search every airline out of Denver. I looked at the ones that were leaving from the earliest moment I could get there after my game on the night of the twenty-third until the morning of the twenty-fifth. Not only could I not find a flight, but there's a storm coming in, and they're guessing all the people who actually did find flights will be sitting at the airport, not flying."

No, he really hated the itchiness of scruff. That was something he was only willing to do when his team made the playoffs. He had to find a razor.

"This sucks," Laura said. "Did you really not have a clue that they were going to trade you?"

"None. I thought things were going well." A lot of trades happened right before the trade deadline, which was in early March this year. If trades happened earlier in the season, it was often because they didn't think a player was a good fit on the team or because the team in general was struggling.

But Connor got along great with his team. He loved the guys. Traveling with them day in and day out, battling with them, shooting for the same goals— he was willing to do anything for them. And his team was doing great. He'd been told by the management not long ago that he was in the team's long-term plans. They'd even put up a billboard featuring him six weeks ago and stocked more of his jerseys in fan stores.

"I was changing after practice when the public relations guy came in and said that the GM wanted to see me." The sinking feeling he'd gotten in his stomach at the time had immediately told him that it was about a trade.

He grabbed a razor and tossed it into his basket, then added some shaving cream.

"Okay," Laura said, "I've got your favorite pajama pants and a few shirts, including that bluish-gray one with the super soft fabric. What else?"

"Shoes." He headed to the next aisle over.

"I can't believe they would actually trade a player eight days before Christmas. Right before the Christmas blackout— which is far too short, if you ask me. No one wants to move across the country at Christmastime, let alone move with no warning."

"It's all part of the life I signed up for when I joined the NHL. At least I don't have a wife and kids I had to break the news to."

"True. But do they really have to give you zero

notice? They couldn't have just selected a later flight today to at least give you a bit of time?"

"You're really hung up on that no-notice thing. It's just part of the job. It sucks, but I've been luckier than most to have spent my entire career up until now near family. Besides, they had press interviews lined up for me, so I had to fly in quickly." He added deodorant to his basket.

"Which they lined up *after* choosing your flight."

"Laura, what's done is done."

"And moaning about it won't change anything," she said, finishing their step-dad's mantra. "I know. How did the interviews go?"

It was more than just interviews. He'd also fielded a dozen messages and calls from his new organization to find out things like his skate size, any sponsored equipment brands, and his number so they could put it on home and away jerseys. He also got calls from the team doctors and training staff to coordinate and get information, and from the Director of Services to make the transition smooth and cover all the bases. He even got a call from payroll.

And that was just the urgent stuff that directly involved him, not any of the stuff going on behind the scenes with media relations, marketing, social media, retail, community relations, and a host of other departments. He wasn't through getting calls, either. Two had come in just in the few minutes he had been on the phone with his sister.

"Fine. I had my suit and dress shoes with me at the arena, of course. Oh, by the way, one of the guys is driving my car back to my place, so don't freak out if he comes in to drop off the keys while you're there. Anyway, the interviews went well, if you don't count how weird it felt to wear dress shoes without socks, which I did *not* happen to grab."

"Oh, socks!" Laura said, followed by sounds of drawers opening and closing.

"Bottom drawer," he offered.

"Got them! Who puts their socks in the bottom drawer? Weirdo. What else? Any bathroom stuff other than your contact lenses?"

"No. I'm not going to wait for that box to be delivered before I brush my teeth or put on deodorant." Toothbrush. That's what he needed. He started walking toward the aisle with them. "You are going to ship it overnight to the hotel, right?"

"Yeah, as soon as I leave here. But in case you've acclimated to the time zone there in the past few hours and already forgot, it's ten p.m. here, so it's not going to be *tonight's* overnight." After a short pause, she added, "So, you might want to find a store where you can buy some underwear, too."

Frustration hit him and came out in a growl. He

tossed a tube of toothpaste into his basket and moved over to the toothbrushes. The shock still hadn't completely worn off yet, but grief and irritation were starting to settle in.

"You couldn't have just refused the trade?"

"Not if I didn't want to be suspended and lose my salary." Another few weeks, and he would've hit his twenty-seventh birthday, and in four months, the end of his seventh year. After hitting either, he could've negotiated a *No trade to Denver* clause in his contract.

Trades were all part of the job, and he'd long ago accepted that a trade at any time, inconvenient or not, was to be expected. It wasn't that he was angry about the timing. Although, he wished they would have waited until December twenty-seventh— when the Christmas trade freeze lifted— to take him away from his family. He was more upset that they traded him to Denver, specifically.

He chose a toothbrush and added it to his basket.

"Well, congrats on getting Mom and Max notified before your trade was officially announced."

Sometimes the players themselves didn't get notified before the media, so the congrats was well-deserved. "I knew she would *not* be happy if she found out from the Internet, so I called her as I was walking out of the GM's office."

"How did it go?"

He swallowed. "I can't say it was fun making her that sad." Christmas traditions were important to her, and he knew that all the ones he was going to miss had likely been running through her head. And he hadn't even let her know the flight situation yet that wouldn't allow him to go home during the three-day break.

"I bet."

"Hey, don't tell Mom that I'm upset about the trade or that I really didn't want to come here. I'll get over being upset, and there isn't anything any of us can do about the trade being to Denver. I don't want her to feel bad."

"I won't. This is just a new adventure, right?" He could tell that she had tried to make the sentence come out in a cheery voice, and she was mostly successful.

"Yep. A new adventure. Oh, and will you take everyone's presents with you to pass out on Christmas morning? And will you wrap Max's for me? I didn't get a chance."

"Will do. Maybe we can just video chat on Christmas as everyone opens presents." There was a small pause before she added, "Okay, I think I've got the necessities, including charging cords for your devices. I'll come back after I get this shipped off and pack more of your stuff. Any last requests for the overnight one? That cinnamon caramel hot chocolate that you love?"

Connor chuckled. "I think I can go a few days without it."

"It's weird to think that this morning when we got together for breakfast, you lived here in Charlotte, were one of the Thunderstorm, and had no idea you'd end the day as one of the Glaciers, living in Denver."

"Yep, weird." It felt like this morning had happened days ago. Waking up, going about his normal routine, going to practice, finding out he was moving fifteen hundred miles away, making that move, fielding all the phone calls, messages, interviews, and emails, coordinating with the new team, and shopping for the essentials was exhausting. He couldn't have stuffed more into this day if he'd tried.

Yet, his new team was on the ice against another team right now, and he wished he was there, playing with them. He glanced at his watch. Actually, the game was probably over by now. It would be nice to have a practice with the new team before a game, and his flight hadn't landed with enough time for him to get to the game, but it still felt strange to have tonight off. Especially because he had tomorrow night off, too— he didn't play his first game with the Glaciers until two days from now.

Someone turned down Connor's aisle, and he could tell the moment the man recognized him because the man's expression turned sour. So, either he recognized

Connor as a Thunderstorm player— and therefore was from the team that was the Glaciers' biggest rival— or the guy already saw the news that Connor had joined the Glaciers, and he wasn't happy about it. He was sure this wasn't going to be an isolated incident.

Connor had pictured being traded plenty of times, but never to Denver. The trade had completely blindsided him. He should've guessed the feelings that coming back would give him. He got it every time his team had played the Glaciers in Denver.

He glanced around the drug store to see if there was anything he needed that he hadn't thought of yet, and luckily, he noticed the shampoo.

"You might not have time to go house shopping," Laura said. "Want me to look through listings and send you the best ones? I can watch for homes with walls that resist puck and stick scuffs. Or one with a trophy room. Swimming pool? An oversized garage with goalie nets and reinforced windows that can handle a hockey puck flying at them?"

"No need. The hotel they've got me at is pretty decent. I'm thinking of living there until the end of the season, then moving back home in the off-season."

"Off-season? If your team does well in the playoffs, that's what? Three months? You can't spend the other nine in a hotel."

"Laura, I am *not* going to live here again." He was

surprised at how fiercely his voice came out. There were too many bad memories tied to this place, and he really didn't like who he was when he lived here. He wasn't about to become that person again. "I'm going to put in a trade request as we come up on the end of the season. I already told my agent."

He headed over to the self-checkout station and started scanning his items. But he couldn't seem to get his mind to go down a different path. So, he asked, "Have you talked to Dad lately? Do you know if he's living here?"

"I haven't for a year or so, but I don't think so. Last I heard, he was living in Arizona and buying a house in Spain."

At least there was that small mercy. Judging by the relief it gave him to know, maybe it wasn't *so* small. "And there's a chance I won't be living in a hotel for the whole season. I could get traded at the deadline to a team that's closer to home."

"Or to one that doesn't get a quarter of their flights delayed due to weather in the winter. Yes, I did, indeed, just look it up."

"Yes, traded to a team without winter flight delays. That'll do, too." He finished scanning the last of his items and tapped his credit card on the reader.

"Then, I'll keep my fingers crossed that you'll get

completely blindsided and have to move with zero notice again soon."

"I always knew I could count on you, sis." He grabbed his bag and noticed that there was a clothing store across the street. It was getting pretty late, but it looked like they were still open. "I've got to go. I need underwear and a shower, and I've got to be at the rink early to meet my new team who was likely just as blindsided by the trade as I was."

"Someone on the Team Services staff can't get that for you? I thought they were there to make the transition smooth."

"I am *not* asking them to buy me underwear."

Laura laughed. "Fair enough. Okay, I'll go get this box shipped. And Connor? Fake it until you make it, right?"

He nodded and smiled. "Fake it until you make it." It was old advice, but there was something to it. Back in college, his hockey coach had their entire team read a book about how body language caused emotions, not the other way around. Slumping made you feel defeated; feeling defeated didn't make you slump. So as a team, they would do winning poses before going on the ice to pump themselves up, and Connor witnessed over and over how much it worked.

It was advice that he'd desperately needed at the time. From a therapy standpoint, if there was an underlying problem, pretending it wasn't there wasn't likely to fix it. But he'd done the therapy, yet he'd still been angry so much of the time back then. The therapy had helped, but it was taking that book to heart that had gotten him past the anger and on his way to becoming the person he was now. A person he liked.

Right now, he just needed to make his body show happiness, and his emotions would follow. So he stood with his shoulders back, put a smile on his face, then crossed the street to the clothing store.

The men's underwear section wasn't hard to find— the four full-size mannequins wearing nothing but underwear, each in a different color, led the way.

He was standing next to a table of underwear packages, finding the style and the size he needed, when a couple of people caught his attention and he glanced over. It was two boys and a girl, all about seventeen years old. One might've been her boyfriend. Or possibly brother.

Connor tried to pretend he didn't notice them as the trio discussed whether the girl should approach Connor and ask for an autograph (since she was a fan and seemed so excited to see him), or if they should maybe hurl insults at "the enemy" instead (which was apparently what the two boys thought of Connor). He wished he was doing anything other than buying underwear at that moment.

Apparently, the girl won the argument, because she straightened her shoulders as if to summon bravery—maybe she read the book, too— and walked over to him with a shy smile. "Hi. You're Connor Greene, right? The hockey player?"

He nodded, and she let out a nervous laugh.

"I think you're a great player." She pulled a Sharpie from her purse. "Can I get your autograph?"

"Sure," he said. "Um, what would you like me to sign?"

The girl looked around like a piece of paper would materialize from somewhere. When it didn't, she picked up one of the packages of underwear. "How about this?"

He hadn't fully formed in his mind the sentence that would suggest they instead ask a cashier if she had a piece of paper before the two guys must've decided that the girl had not, in fact, won the debate. They both grabbed unpackaged underwear from a bin, wadded them up, and hurled them at Connor.

The girl turned to the boys, shouted, "Losers!" then stormed off as they continued throwing underwear at him. He wasn't sure if he'd rather they hurled the insults. At least the underwear was quieter.

They were relentless, though. He turned away from the flying underwear balls to make a quick escape toward the doors and ran right into a woman. He had been in such a hurry to leave that his speed knocked them both off their feet. He wrapped his arms around the woman as they fell, twisting so that he would land on the bottom instead of landing on her.

Which wouldn't have been so bad, except that they hit a mannequin on the way down, knocking it over. And as it fell, it took out the next mannequin, which took out the next one. Connor, the woman, and each of the four mannequins fell to the ground like dominos. The landing knocked the air right out of him.

His sister was right— he really should've let someone from team services buy the underwear.

three

KATIE PUSHED the door of the department store in Denver open and walked inside, her eyes finding the hanging sign overhead for the men's department before going back to the contract on her phone that she'd received from the legal department at the Glaciers. She was scanning it trying to find any clauses related to specific dates as she made her way back to the section where she was hoping to find some funny socks for her brother-in-law, Cory.

The spot for the name of the player she would be filming was blank, which was the source of the problem. Her dad had called to tell her about getting selected for this job weeks ago, and she really thought she'd know who her assigned player was long before now. Other videographers got their player's names right away and were able to schedule events earlier in the month when things weren't so tightly packed with Christmas.

She had even started seeing ads from the Glaciers using footage that other videographers had sent in. The ads usually cut between clips of two or three players, each being helpful with some Christmas activity in some town. Every time she saw one, it stressed her out that she didn't even know who she was supposed to be filming yet.

And she was no longer sure how she was going to fit everything in. She already had scheduled videography jobs coming up with a couple of families to film their Christmas parties, as well as her own family's traditions, and filming and editing the video she created for them.

Not to mention the stress she was feeling about the possibility that anything she filmed would get to the Glaciers too late for them to even use. And then what if it caused the Glaciers to lose faith in her and not want to use her for anything ever again? Plus, there was a player out there who wasn't going to get much screen time if things didn't start happening soon.

She was going to her parents' house tomorrow night for their annual Santa Hat activity, though, and her dad had promised that everything would be set in stone by then, and he would let her know who her player was at the activity.

She skimmed past a lot of information on what types

of things she should film, how many separate activities, and how much footage she would need to send to the team to be compiled into their campaign. There was an entire section that said they had editing rights and that anything could be cut, which she expected.

It included a player confidentiality clause that basically stated that if she discovered something personal about a player that they didn't want disclosed, she couldn't disclose it. She also couldn't film him looking like a jerk. Probably because the purpose of this campaign was to raise the team's image, not to make it worse. So, hopefully, the player she got assigned wasn't a jerk.

Something hit Katie in the chest and then fell onto her phone. She picked it up to see that it was a new pair of wadded-up men's underwear. Her head jerked up, her eyes searching for the underwear's origination, and saw a big guy standing right in front of her. Two teenage boys a dozen feet away immediately sent another wadded-up pair through the air, tagging the man in the shoulder.

He spun around to make an escape, but unfortunately, his exit route led exactly where she stood and he knocked into her. Her breath escaped with a whoosh as the two of them fell toward the floor. She wasn't sure how it happened, since he hit into her, but he managed to twist in mid-air so that when they landed, she was on top of him and was suddenly chest-to-chest with a large, muscular man.

She drew in a quick breath to replace the one that had been knocked out of her as her attention jerked to the mannequins that were crashing to the ground, one after another.

It was a moment before the shock of getting knocked down and of all the mannequins falling before it sunk in that she was laying on top of a man, his strong arms wrapped around her. And then another second before her eyes made it to the man's face. And about one more for recognition to dawn on her, and then she narrowed her eyes.

It was Connor Greene. He was the one player that Katie knew on sight even without a lesson from Emmalee. Everyone in Mountain Springs knew him— the right wing for the Charlotte Thunderstorm, which was who the Glaciers must've played tonight if he was in town. A lot of people saw him as the golden boy who went from a small-town hockey rink to the National Hockey League. Of course, those people were always the ones who *didn't* go to high school with him. If they had, they'd know he was a jerk.

Like he was at Katie's very first high school dance. She'd been wearing a dress she'd borrowed from her older sister, Noelle— a dress she'd promised she would return in the same condition she borrowed it in. Connor was at the dance, too, and decided to pick a fight with someone. Before long, more than a dozen people were involved, and Connor crashed into the punch table, sending almost the entire bowl of punch onto Katie, soaking her from head to toe in a very staining red liquid. The entire school lost school dance privileges for four months because of the brawl.

She pushed herself off the man as the boys threw a last couple of pairs of underwear before running off. Katie got to her feet as Connor was pushing himself to a sitting position. She had seen a picture or two of Connor since that day in the high school gym, but she hadn't seen him in person. It caught her off guard how good-looking he'd become.

Not that becoming more eye-pleasing on the outside changed anything. She put a hand on her hip. "Well, it looks like not much has changed. People still want to throw stuff at you."

She caught a glimpse of confusion on his face before she turned on her heel, leaving him in her dust as she exited the store.

THE NEXT EVENING, Katie pulled up in front of her parents' extremely decorated home in Mountain Springs. Even though it wasn't quite 6:00 yet, it was already dark, making the explosion of lights over the entire house, on every tree, and lighting up every decoration in every area on their big front lawn even more impressive. There was a part with a large nativity complete with all the animals, another with Santa's village, an area with giant Christmas tree ornaments, and a group of nearly life-size carolers.

Before she got out of the car, she sent a text to Emmalee.

Katie: I'm sad you're not here with me for Santa Hat night!

Emmalee: I am sad, too!

Although to be honest, I was a little intimidated by the whole thing and was kind of wishing there was someone you'd want to take as a date.

Katie: Emmalee! Did your grandpa really fall? Or was that just an excuse not to come save me?

Emmalee: He really did fall. And I really was the only one close enough to get him to the hospital. No way I would've left you high and dry without a good excuse. Are you sure there isn't someone you could ask as your date with zero notice?

> Katie: Nope. I'm just going to be on my own solo team. It's going to be awesome.

It wasn't going to be awesome. It wasn't the type of thing one would ever choose to do solo. Maybe her family would give her a five-minute head start as the only unmarried, couldn't-get-a-date sibling.

She walked into the just as elaborately-decorated inside and hugged her mom, her very pregnant sister, Noelle, and Noelle's husband, Jack. Then she hugged her sisters, Becca, Hope, and Julianne, along with their husbands and a total of ten nieces and nephews. And her parents' black lab, Captain. And in the process, she confirmed at least three times that she was, indeed, there without a date.

Her dad walked out of his office down the hall, a phone to his ear, and from what she could hear over the sound of everyone, she guessed it was a work call he was finishing up. Since she had a moment, she sent a quick text to Emmalee that she'd been meaning to send. Katie had videoed a wedding proposal last night in the pine trees and snow at the edge of town and didn't see Emmalee before she went to bed. And then with the craziness of Emmalee's grandpa falling, she had somehow forgotten to tell her best friend about what happened last night.

> Katie: So, I'm guessing the Glaciers played the Charlotte Thunderstorm last night? Because guess who I ran into — or, I should say, guess who ran into me — in the men's underwear section at a department store in Denver?
>
> Connor Greene!

She pressed send, imagining what Emmalee's reaction would be just as her dad hung up the phone and called everyone to gather around. Maybe she should've waited to tell Emmalee the story because she wasn't going to get a chance to respond for a bit. She did glance at her phone when a text from Emmalee came in, though.

> Emmalee: The Glaciers played the Washington Hydra last night…

Katie was still furrowing her brow in confusion at Emmalee's text when her dad started talking.

"Before we get started on our annual Santa Hat competition, I have a few announcements I need to make. Katie, this first one is mostly for you."

Katie perked up, remembering that she was going to find out which player she would be videoing tonight.

"The reason why we couldn't tell you which player was yours sooner is because the GM told me they were working on a trade. I knew you could handle getting started a little late with the player who Mountain Springs was getting, so I had the new player assigned here. The trade took longer than they expected, though, which gives you a much smaller window to get all the filming done. I'm really sorry about that."

A smaller time frame to do the filming, she could handle. But *a new player*? It felt like a stone had just dropped into Katie's stomach. She glanced at the phone that was still in her hand.

"Anyway, the trade went through, and the new player flew in last night. If any players had a connection with any particular town in Colorado, we tried to assign them to that area. I assumed that the new player we'd get wouldn't have a connection to anywhere in Colorado, but... Surprise!"

No, no, no.

"He actually does have a connection with Mountain Springs! Noelle, I think that you might have gone to school with him. It's Connor Greene!"

Julianne's husband, Ben, and Becca's husband, Corbin, high-fived each other. Cory pumped his fist and said, "Yes!" Most of the kids were jumping up and cheering, even though— except for maybe three or four of them— they had no idea what they were cheering for. They were just excited about group excitement. Jack looked to Noelle to gauge her reaction, while all five sisters looked at each other. The four of them had the same wary expression on their faces that Katie knew she wore.

Actually, hers was much more than wariness. She wasn't even sure what it was, because a mix of many emotions was swirling through her. None of them good. All of which made her feel both tense and twitchy at the same time. And, oddly enough, made her jaw feel tight.

Her dad continued talking, although a little more cautiously, as if trying to figure out the mix of positive and negative emotions he was sensing. "He practiced with the team today, and I had a good chat with him after, where I explained about going to a town to do Christmas events for a video. He seems like a good guy. I asked him about his Christmas plans, and he was really feeling bad that he wouldn't be able to go home for Christmas because of the storm coming in and the lack of flights."

Katie mentally crossed all her fingers and toes, silently hoping that the next words out of her dad's mouth wouldn't be what she could guess they would be.

"So, I talked to your mom, and we decided to invite him to stay with us over the three-day break they get for Christmas."

And there it was. The person in all of her high school — all grades included— that she liked least of all was going to be invading their family Christmas.

"So, Katie, I guess it was a good thing that your plans

for a teammate for this activity fell through because I have someone else for you to partner up with."

"What?" Katie nearly shouted as a knock sounded on the front door. "Dad, please tell me that you didn't invite him to come tonight."

"Why? I thought it would be a great chance for the two of you to get to know each other before you have to start filming him. It might make it easier to, you know, dig deep in your video and show the real Connor. Since he's new to the team, it'll give fans a chance to connect with him more. Oh, and there's the man of the hour right there!"

Katie's dad held out his arm and she turned to see the tall, muscular man who had crashed into her at the department store.

This was a nightmare come to life.

He'd started strolling into the room looking plenty confident, but as his eyes roved the room, his stride became more hesitant. It seemed like he was gathering puzzle pieces and slowly snapping them together. And then his eyes fell on Katie, and she could swear that she could actually see color leaving his face. His feet shifted ever so slightly, and she could tell at that moment that a part of him wanted to turn around and leave and that all of him was suddenly regretting saying yes to her dad's offer.

Instead, though, he walked all the way up to her dad,

shook his hand, then shook her mom's hand and thanked them for inviting him.

Her nerve endings seemed to tingle at seeing both the strong, confident walk and the slight show of vulnerability. Why? Why? Why wasn't her body getting the memo that she didn't like him? This man was a jerk in high school. Why the fluttering?

It was probably because when he knocked into her at the department store, he had twisted to make sure he fell first, protecting her. She was just feeling that. Protection appreciation. Nothing else.

Her dad started introducing him to everyone. When he got to Noelle, Connor said, "We went to high school together, right?"

"Yep. We had U.S. History together for the first half of our junior year."

Connor kept a smile on his face, but Katie could see the wince behind it, too. Then her dad motioned to her. "And this is my daughter, Katie."

Connor shook her hand, but the guy's face was pretty easy to read, so she could tell that he was racking his brain, trying to figure out if he knew her in high school.

"You don't remember me, do you?"

"From last night?"

She ignored the raised eyebrows from practically everyone else in the room. "No, from high school." She paused when there was still no recognition in his expression. "I was a freshman at that Christmas dance."

Connor didn't ask which one— they both knew which dance she was referring to. It was a low blow to bring it up, but also, it was oddly satisfying to see the look on his face.

Connor dipped his head a bit and scratched the back of his neck. "I'm really sorry about that."

Her dad didn't seem to know which dance they were talking about, and she didn't expect him to. He had five daughters, so there were a *lot* of school dances. She could tell that he sensed the awkwardness yet needed to press on anyway. "I'm glad you're here and have been introduced— again, apparently— because Katie, here, is the videographer that is assigned to you for the Christmas player promotions I told you about earlier today."

The new expression that crossed Connor Greene's face? That one was even better.

CONNOR

TODAY, Connor got to be on the ice with his new team in Denver and was introduced to everyone. Most players in the NHL had experienced either getting traded or having a teammate they were good friends with get traded. Everyone, himself included, accepted that it was just part of the game. They always embraced the new guy because they understood how hard a trade was on a player. Connor had done it plenty of times with players traded to the Thunderstorm.

But even though the Glaciers embraced him and welcomed him onto the team, he still got the sense that they weren't entirely happy about the trade. Which was probably pretty common. He'd felt the same about new players to his own team plenty of times.

He didn't know the details of their feelings about his

trade, specifically, though, and didn't know anyone well enough yet to ask. Although, one player, Erik Henderson, seemed like a cool guy. And another player, Briggs, seemed particularly unhappy about Connor's presence.

Connor reminded himself that it was all temporary. He'd get traded closer to home soon. Maybe before the trade deadline in March, but for sure by summer. He wanted to gel with the team until then, but he didn't want to get comfortable.

After practice, he met with Reid Allred and immediately liked the guy. He worked with players and their agents to discuss branding themselves and the team and each player's role on the team. So he'd be working with him off and on while he was with the Glaciers.

Then, Mr. Allred explained that they'd had a few players on the team who wreaked havoc on the team's image, harming ticket sales, especially for families. They'd traded a couple of players in the off-season, but the player they had just traded for Connor had caused a lot of damage by his actions both on and off the ice, and they were working on repairing that image.

Image repair was a pretty normal part of life for a team. So was having the players do things in the communities where they played. Being assigned to a community to do at least three activities in the week leading up to Christmas, which also happened to be your very first week on the team, was not so normal. Especially when they also had three games between now and then. It helped that the guy acknowledged that it would be a challenge for him and was apologetic about it.

It also helped that the guy recognized that Connor would be away from family for Christmas and offered to let him stay with his family during the three days he'd be off for Christmas. He probably should've guessed that there would be a problem going to someone's home if they lived in Mountain Springs.

Mr. Allred just looked so much younger than Connor's step-dad that he'd assumed the man's daughters would be younger— the ages where they'd still be living at home, not that they'd be his age.

And he definitely didn't expect to show up at Mr. Allred's house and see the woman he'd plowed into last night at the department store. Sure, she was extremely attractive and he felt like he'd connected with her a teeny bit, and not in an "accidentally crashed into her physically" kind of way. But the whole experience had been embarrassing in so many ways that he'd hoped that he'd never run into her again.

When she'd made the comment about people still wanting to throw things at him, he had assumed it was a hockey thing, especially since he came from the Thunderstorm. He hadn't recognized her from high school at all. Even after finding out he'd known her from there, he still had no flash of recognition.

His parents had a plethora of problems in his sophomore and junior years of high school, so most of his high school memories were of that. Apparently, he'd only focused on his own problems and not on anyone else at all. He might have only been in high school with two of these sisters, but by the way all five looked at him, they all knew about him.

And he had already agreed to stay with them over Christmas. Was it too late to back out?

They didn't leave any time for stewing in the awkwardness, though, before Mrs. Allred pulled out a Santa hat and said, "Are you all ready to get started?"

Everyone shouted yes, the kids most animated of all. Even the black lab seemed excited about it. Connor leaned in toward Katie and asked, "What are we about to do?" And just like last night, when they had fallen, he felt a current run through him at the nearness. A tingle of nerve endings. It was almost as if she exuded an electric charge and by getting close, he was bound to feel it.

She turned her head to him, eyes still on the Santa hat like she didn't want to miss anything, and said, "Each sibling is a team with their family. My parents are a team, too." Her eyes met his. "You're my team, by the way. We didn't get off on the right foot in high school, and we didn't again last night. But just so you know, we're going to win this."

He smiled at her conviction. He was definitely down for winning.

"We each pull out an assignment— two people get entertainment, which is a skit; two people get decorations; and two people get dinner. Except it's not that straight-forward. There are obstacles and a time limit and a money limit, and you're competing against the other team that drew the same thing."

Connor nodded. Sitting around, socializing with people who only knew him as who he used to be sounded like torture. A competition, he could handle. And as much as he didn't want to be surrounded by people who didn't have the best opinions of him, it felt good to be around a family, even if it wasn't his own, doing family Christmas things. Tonight, his family was decorating the big tree, and he was missing it.

The oldest sister, Becca, if he remembered correctly, drew a paper out of the Santa hat that Mrs. Allred held, and read, "Decorations!" Everyone reacted loudly. This was a group that really seemed to like cheering. It almost sounded like a hockey game in here.

"There are a lot of details to it," Katie continued. "We don't need to worry about all that right now. What we need to worry about is not drawing *Dinner*."

"Why do we need to worry about that?"

Another sister drew out "Entertainment!" and everyone cheered again.

"Let's just say that every other time I've drawn dinner, bad things happened."

Her sister, Noelle, the one he'd gone to school with, drew out "Dinner!" and again with the clapping and hooting, but this time with a breath of relief from Katie, probably because it just cut down their chances of pulling a dinner paper from the hat, too.

"Like what?" he asked.

"Oh, you know, just things like forgetting a pan of garlic bread was in the oven on broil until the smoke started pouring out, forgetting to put any kind of liquid in the Instant Pot when using it as a pressure cooker, a completely inedible pasta sauce. Once I forgot to turn on the burner for the eggs, realized it at the last moment, and put them in the microwave instead.

"Another time, I dropped a big pot of soup on the way to the table, sending it everywhere. And I do mean *everywhere.* Adding a bit too much salt, making everyone say 'I'm headed into the salt mines' with every bite they took. Setting a hot pad on fire. Things like that. Some of those things happened in the same year, obviously. I haven't actually drawn the 'Dinner' paper that many times."

He chuckled. "Okay then, we are crossing our fingers for 'entertainment' or 'decorations.'"

"Either one."

Another sister pulled out *Decorations*, leaving just

Katie and her parents to draw, and if he remembered correctly, that meant there was one for entertainment and one for dinner remaining. And, of course, she drew out the paper that read *Dinner*. And, of course, everyone groaned.

He watched Katie as she narrowed her eyes at the little strip of paper like she was challenging it. Then, when her dad said, "You've got five minutes to discuss with your team, and then we'll start the timer. Go!" Katie grabbed hold of his hand and pulled him to a small room off the kitchen with a washer and dryer.

She closed the door and met his eyes with her very fierce ones. She was standing close in the small space, so he got a good look at those eyes. They were blue at the outer rim with gold around the pupil, and her eyes were framed by dark eyelashes. As far as eyes went, they were rather mesmerizing. He could imagine himself getting very easily pulled in by those eyes. But he wasn't going to be in Colorado long enough for that to happen.

Besides, he didn't want to be with someone who knew him as who he used to be. It hadn't been easy for him to become who he was now, and he expected it was just as difficult for anyone who knew him back then to think of him any differently.

"Okay, here's the deal," she said. "We have a budget and thirty minutes to shop for food and get back here to meet the other team. They'll take the food we bought and we take theirs. Then we each have thirty minutes to make something out of those ingredients. The team who makes the best meal wins."

"Oof. That doesn't sound easy."

"It's not. But we *have* to win this," she said. "It's really important."

He didn't know if she was always this competitive, but he liked it. He found himself nodding and getting pumped up for the challenge. "So what's the best strategy?"

"We buy about ten items for them and they buy ten for us. The trick is to buy foods that aren't gross. Unlike the year when Julianne's team bought anchovies, wasabi peas, sprouted wheat cinnamon raisin bread, and a cheese that smelled like feet, and Becca's team made grilled cheese out of it. Because we are all going to eat what the other team makes, so we want it edible. But we also want to win, so we want to pick things that don't naturally go well together."

A smile was spreading across his face as he imagined it. They only had thirty minutes, so they'd have to race through the grocery store, but he was sure they'd be able to pick some things that would give the other team the bigger challenge. "This is going to be fun."

"Thirty seconds," they heard Mr. Allred's muffled voice call out from the kitchen.

Katie side-eyed him. "Okay, you're looking a little too

excited right now. You aren't going to start throwing any punches, are you?"

He winked. "Nah. I save that for high school dances."

Once Mr. Allred called out that the competition had begun, he and Katie raced outside and they both got into her car. She said it had been too long since he had practiced driving on snow-packed roads— even though he'd driven to the Allred's house fine— and probably didn't remember where the grocery store was. For the record: he did. But he would've been fine letting her drive if she'd simply said she wanted to.

The seven-minute drive to the grocery store was great because they spent the time brainstorming which items to get. They decided on hot dogs (after debating whether they should be considered "gross," and he thought about how they would affect his hockey performance), quinoa, spaghetti noodles, root beer, creamed corn, a can of cranberry sauce, radishes, and Greek yogurt.

Once they got there, they raced through the store to grab everything while he added up the prices on his phone. They still had a few dollars left after grabbing the final item and since they hadn't made it to ten items yet, they threw in some pretzels and gummy worms. The checkout line ate five precious minutes, but they managed to hop into the car with a full eight minutes left.

The drive back to the Allred's house was less great. No brainstorming was needed since they wouldn't know what foods they had to work with until they returned, so the awkwardness of realizing he was in a room with people who had experienced the high school version of himself returned.

And for some reason, Connor wanted to win Katie over. Why? He wasn't sure. He knew it wasn't because she would be videoing him, and it wasn't because he normally had a need to win people over. But it was there, and he decided that the only way to get past it was to address the elephant in the room— the school dance.

"Can I explain about the dance?"

"Connor, you don't need to explain about the dance."

"I know. But can I anyway?" He wasn't the same person that he was in high school, and he was pretty sure that she was still seeing him as that guy. She nodded, and he suddenly wished he would've thought through what, exactly, he wanted to share. But since he hadn't, he just started talking and hoped for the best.

"My parents' marriage started going downhill my sophomore year of high school, and I really struggled with it. But not as much as I did at the beginning of my junior year when my dad left. Just before he did, he pulled me and my sister aside and said that his leaving didn't have anything to do with us and that he still wanted to see us all the time. Typical divorce stuff, I guess. But it didn't take long before he was off, living his best life, forgetting about us completely. I didn't handle that so well and kind of became a hotheaded idiot."

That was an understatement. He'd been so bitter and angry about not only not having his dad around, but also seeing what it was doing to his mom. He was hurting and showed it by acting out a lot, catching so many people in the crossfire.

Why was he telling this to Katie? The fact that there were circumstances that led to the state of mind he was in at the time didn't change the fact that he did what he did. Maybe he was telling her so that he was more than the memory of a kid who made bad choices. So she got that there was more to him. And for some reason, he really wanted her to see the real him.

Katie kept her eyes on the road, but she nodded slightly, and he could tell that she was paying very close attention to his words so he continued. "I was in a club hockey league with other high school players in our county. Trav Donovan was in the same league, but we were on different teams. We were both captains and didn't like each other much. But I especially didn't like him when he asked my little sister, Laura, to the Christmas dance."

Katie glanced at him for a second before her eyes were back on the road. "The fight started with the two of you?"

"Yep. He came over and made a hurtful, if not clever or unique, comment about how he'd heard that my mom didn't have a big, strong man at the house anymore and asked if he needed to step in. Given the state I was in at the time, that alone probably would've been enough to provoke a fight with me. But then he said something crude about what he was going to show my sister later that night.

"Not that it was any excuse— there are plenty of kids who experience the same things with their parents that I did, and then have someone talk crap about their mom or sister, but they *don't* get their school's dance privileges taken away for four months.

"And I don't know if he was just trying to bait me or not. In his defense, I was easy to bait back then. So, I threw the first punch. Everyone kind of assumed that we were fighting as captains of two different hockey teams, so anyone at the dance who was also on one of our teams joined in and turned it into an all-out brawl."

"That was why so many people joined in so quickly?"

Connor grimaced. "Mostly. Trav and I also both played on the high school baseball team, so all those players joined in, too."

Katie stopped at a stop sign, looked both ways, then said, "And none of them thought to ask what the fight was even about?"

He chuckled. "Listen, most high school boys who are

dealing with some crap in their life need a reason to fight, but they don't necessarily need to know the reason. I don't know if I was glad for the support, or if I was just in my own troubled world so much that I didn't even care what else was going on.

"But the worst part about it was that someone gave me a good hit to the gut, and it made me back into the refreshment table. I was so mad that I shoved off that table to go after the guy, completely toppling it over. I spun around just in time to see the punch bowl go flying and dowse some poor girl."

Katie raised her hand. "Hi. That was me."

His eyes went wide. "You're joking."

She shook her head as she turned onto her parents' street. "I was soaked from the top of my head to the toes of my heels."

Connor ran his hands over his face and then around again until his fingers were steepled at the top of his nose. No way that after ten years, chance brought him into the same car with the recipient of the punch bowl that his anger had sent flying, at Christmastime, even. To add to it, that person was going to soon be videoing him as a hockey player with his new team. Was this what being mortified felt like?

He removed his hands from his face as she pulled into the driveway. "I am so sorry."

"Connor, it's okay. It was a long time ago. Besides, it

wasn't even my dress that got ruined— I had borrowed it from my sister."

"I think that makes it even worse. Okay, we are going to win this contest for you. Right now."

Katie nodded once as she put the car into park. "I'm down for that."

"What's at stake?"

"Officially? A trophy that we get to keep for a year, along with bragging rights. Unofficially? A curse lifted and future smack talk about me drawing the 'Dinner' paper abated."

He glanced over at Noelle and Jack, the couple who were competing against them, as they pulled into the driveway next to them. Then he turned back to Katie. "Okay, we're doing this."

KATIE

THIS WAS PROBABLY the seventh time that Katie had done the Santa Hat activity with a date as her partner. But as they hurried to grab out the bags of groceries, laughing and bumping shoulders with Noelle and Jack as the four of them all tried to go through the door first, she realized it was the first time she was going into it with confidence that her teammate was as dedicated to winning as she was. Maybe they actually had a chance.

For a moment, she internally rolled her eyes at the thought. She'd chosen the *Dinner* paper, after all. Maybe if they'd drawn anything else. She never would've guessed that Connor Greene, of all people, would make her feel like she had someone who was very solidly on her team.

They laid out the groceries they bought for Jack and

Noelle to use on one end of the long table. It had all the leaves in it, ready to seat all twenty-two of them. Jack and Noelle set out all the food items they'd bought on the other end. Then they swapped sides to see what they had to work with.

Both she and Connor started moving items around on the table, pulling things together that seemed like they fit, and it didn't take long to see a theme. There was a turkey breast, a big can of pumpkin pie mix, heavy cream, cranberry sauce, and mini marshmallows, like the kind they always put on top of yams. Did Jack & Noelle think they could make a Thanksgiving dinner in — she looked at her watch— twenty-seven minutes? The turkey breast was thawed and boneless and the ovens were both pre-heated, but still, twenty-seven minutes wasn't enough time.

Katie and Connor had chosen for Jack and Noelle a bunch of random ingredients that they didn't think would go together. But Jack and Noelle seemed to be leading them along a theme that they couldn't possibly pull off in the amount of time that they had.

She picked up a head of cauliflower and a bag of Lay's potato chips and, loudly enough to be heard at the other end of the table, said, "Really? Are we supposed to mash potato chips into cauliflower to make it taste like mashed potatoes?"

Noelle patted her pregnant belly and said, "What can

I say? The baby loved Thanksgiving and wants it again. But we're not telling you what you have to make at all. Besides, can you really complain when you gave us..." she picked up two items, "Hot dogs and gummy worms?"

"Fair enough," Katie said, and couldn't help the smile on her face. She was pretty sure that she and Connor had bought some pretty difficult ingredients to use together.

Then, in a quieter voice meant only for Connor, she said, "Seriously, though, how are we supposed to make Thanksgiving dinner in such a short amount of time?" She pulled together the other ingredients that didn't seem to fit the theme— red and green bell peppers, Reese's Puffs cereal, flour tortillas, and a can of pineapple chunks. She couldn't even imagine how to use them.

Connor just looked at the ingredients for a small moment, hands on his hips, a focused expression on his face. Then he said, "The theme is just to throw us off. To keep us from thinking of other things."

Katie eyed her sister and her brother-in-law. "Clever."

He started moving things around, putting them in different groups. "We have pineapple and peppers. Can we use any additional ingredients besides what's here?"

Katie nodded. "Yes. Salt, pepper, seasonings, oils, and

condiments. But we have to use *all* the ingredients they bought for us."

"Okay, we have pineapple chunks. We could make something similar to sweet and sour chicken but use turkey instead. Then we can cut it into small enough chunks to cook in time, and maybe use the cauliflower as rice. To make the sauce, we can use marshmallows instead of brown sugar, some of the juice from the pineapples, and I'm sure your parents have ketchup, soy sauce, and cornstarch."

"Oh, wow," Katie said, feeling a bit impressed and in awe. "You're actually pretty brilliant."

"I can't say that is the most frequent compliment that hockey players tend to get."

Katie picked up the box of cereal, thinking, then grabbed the marshmallows. "Rice Krispies treats!"

Connor paused a second before he grabbed the can of jellied cranberry sauce. "We can use this in the sauce for sugar instead of the marshmallows." Then he grabbed the potato chips. "Maybe crumble some of these up with the Reese's Puffs? It could be a sweet and salty treat."

"I'm not sure if that will make it awful or awfully tasty. I say we find out."

Connor pulled the final two ingredients toward them — the pumpkin pie mix and the flour tortillas— and Katie gasped. "We can make mini pumpkin pies in a muffin tin! We'll use the tortillas as a crust, and we can whip the cream."

"That's perfect." As they quickly gathered all the ingredients into their arms to haul them over to the counters, Connor said, "But we need a side. Our plan gives us one main dish and two desserts."

"We can call the pumpkin pies a side." When Connor shot her a look, she said, "What? Pumpkin is a vegetable, right?"

They were down to twenty-three minutes remaining, so Katie hurried to put a skillet on the stove and turned the burner on, and they quickly divided up who was going to work on what item first. Connor cut the turkey into cubes, dredging them in corn starch and putting them into the skillet as he went, while Katie cut up the peppers on a second cutting board beside him as fast as she could.

"Coming up with what to make out of random ingre-dients is one of the hardest parts of drawing the *Dinner* paper." She glanced at him as she worked. She had to admit that the guy was creative. "Yet you came up with something pretty great."

"Wow. A second compliment in three minutes." He didn't look away from his slicing— which was good, because they were in a hurry— but said, "I guess when your parents start to have a falling out that lasts the better part of a year, then your dad leaves completely and your mom is left dealing with a myriad of struggles, you tend to get plenty of opportunities to figure out how to make things from random ingredients that resemble meals."

Katie did actually stop slicing peppers for a full five seconds to just look at Connor. She wasn't sure what she thought of him, exactly, but she was definitely intrigued. Plus, he had that strong jaw and the hair that curled over his ear just a bit that was rather attractive.

Stop being attracted, Katie, she reminded herself. She had a plan and was going to stick with it.

She finished cutting the peppers before Connor finished the turkey, so she started grating the cauliflower. Her parents had two ovens, but they had to share the stove with Noelle and Jack, so they only got two of the burners. Things were going to get tricky, so she got out another pan to cook and slightly toast the cauliflower.

Before long, Katie found herself cutting the tortillas into triangles and working to get them to sit right in the muffin tin right next to where Noelle was layering Greek yogurt, gummy worms, crushed pretzels, and a drizzle of cranberry sauce in nearly two dozen clear cups at one end of the long island counter. Connor was at the other end, mixing ingredients into a bowl for the sauce, taste-testing it, and then making adjustments. Jack was keeping an eye on... Katie wasn't sure exactly what on the stove while mixing stuff in with the spaghetti.

Without glancing up, Noelle nodded her head toward Connor. "Things between you two don't seem as tense as when he first got here."

Katie used the back of her hand to rub her forehead and took a quick look at Connor. "I can forgive the guy who ruined the dance and my dress."

"*My* dress."

"*Your* dress. It was a very long time ago. What matters is what he's like now."

A bit of yogurt fell from the spoon as Noelle was scooping it, falling onto the apron covering her big belly. Noelle just looked at it, sighed, and kept going. "And what is he like now? Dateable?"

The old her would've said yes. The new her didn't. "I don't have enough info yet."

"But you do think he's very attractive, right?"

Katie smiled. "That, he is." She glanced at him again as he took the sauce to the stove, gave both the cauliflower and the turkey a stir, then added the peppers to the turkey skillet. "As far as the rest goes, though, I'm withholding judgment for now. I'm sure I'll find out what he's really like as we're filming."

"Come on, Katie. He's been great while he's been here. You can't tell me that you haven't been thinking about what it would be like to date him, even if it's only for fun and not for anything long-term."

"Okay, I have." Because he kind of got her heart fluttering quite a bit. She placed the final tortilla triangle in the last of the two muffin tins and grabbed the can of pumpkin pie mix and a can opener. "And I also haven't. I decided I make decisions too quickly when it comes to men to date, and I made a goal to be more skeptical. Now, I slow down and get more information first. I don't use my initial gut reaction anymore. That thing can't be trusted."

She exhaled as she opened the can of pumpkin. "Besides, even if he does end up being great, when would I ever fit in dating? Christmas is in a week. I have to film Connor at three activities. Then I have to edit all that footage and get it sent in."

As she put dollop after dollop of pie filling in each spot in the muffin tin, moving as quickly as she could, all the things she needed to do outside of tonight moved just as quickly through her mind. "I need to finish filming our family's video and edit it, and I have to do one for the Waldrops' Christmas party in a few days, edit that, work at my other job because this time of year is always crazy for Emmalee, and finish last minute shopping. On top of all our regular family traditions. Plus, I don't even really know what he's like yet. And I'll only see him through Christmas, anyway."

"You're right. It's good to know when to admit defeat, call it quits," Noelle said as she drizzled the last bit of cranberry sauce on her crazy creations in a flourish.

"You'll never get me to admit defeat. Like everything, I'm in this to win it." She was pretty sure she was talking about the dinner competition now.

Katie put the mini pumpkin pies in the oven, and then Connor dipped a spoon in the sauce on the stove and held out the spoon. "Taste this. Does it need anything?"

"Oh, wow," Katie said, wiping a bit of sauce off her lip with her knuckle. "That is amazing." He seriously made that using random ingredients and cranberry sauce. Was she impressed? Maybe. Was she going to let herself be attracted, based on that impressiveness? Nope. She was going to stick to her plan.

"What's left to do?" Connor asked.

"Whip the cream and make the Rice Krispies treats." She glanced at her watch. "And we've only got seven minutes left!"

Without discussing what they were each going to do, Katie got out a pot and started melting the butter and marshmallows, and Connor pulled out a bowl and started measuring Reese's Puffs cereal and crushing the potato chips into it. As she mixed the melted marshmallow mixture into the cereal, he whipped the cream.

When she reached for something in his space, he leaned away the perfect amount. When one of them needed a utensil that was closer to the other, they handed it to the other person before they even asked. Almost like they'd rehearsed everything ahead of time.

And it was extra surprising that they were working so well together given the fact that they were working against the clock. She had done the Santa Hat activity with plenty of different dates over the years, so she knew how much the time limit could bring out not only the stress but annoyance with each other.

(Unless they drew the *Entertainment* paper. It was easy to go with the flow when it came to a skit, because no one knew if you were following a script or making it up as you went, anyway. *Dinner*, though? That was a completely different beast.)

As Noelle tended to whatever hotdog concoction they had going on at the other burner, from the corner of her eye, Katie saw that Noelle was smiling at their in-syncedness. If she felt the need to bring it up, Katie could always bring up the "loading frosting bags and getting some on my cheek so he has to wipe it off" incident that happened in this very kitchen between Jack and Noelle that Katie had a front row seat to.

Wait. That eventually led to the two of them getting married, so maybe it wasn't the best comeback.

They were down to almost no time left when she

dumped the Reese's Puffs treats into a pan and the two of them pressed it out together. Katie pulled the remaining bit of it from the spoon she'd used, divided it in half, then put half in her mouth and half in Connor's. Her eyebrows shot up just as Connor said, "Oh! This is actually quite good. I didn't think it would be."

She playfully punched him in the shoulder. "Weren't you the one who suggested it?"

"Yes. I like taking risks. It doesn't mean that they always work out."

With less than a minute to go, they hurried to cut up the treats, which were still too warm to be cut in a pretty way, so it took a little finessing, pulled the mini pies from the oven, and barely had time to get everything on a sample plate to show before the air horn sounded from where her parents were coming up the stairs from the basement. All her siblings, their spouses, and their kids descended on the room that was a combination kitchen, dining room, and family room, all seeming pretty excited about whatever they'd prepared.

Katie took a deep breath and stood next to Connor, but the nerves that had popped up the moment that horn had sounded stuck around. While she and Connor had been cooking, she'd forgotten about her curse when it came to the *Dinner* card. There was one other time she had, too, and that was when she and her partner had spilled the pot of soup everywhere. She leaned in closer to Connor. "If anything needs to be picked up and moved at all, I need you to do it."

He didn't question it— he just nodded and lifted one of the arms crossed over his chest enough to form a fist, so she bumped it with hers. "We've got this," he said.

When she'd leaned in to bump his fist, they'd gotten close enough that her entire upper arm was pressed against his, and she didn't move. It made it feel like they were an unstoppable team. She could really get used to having a teammate who was as dedicated to winning as she was. And had she ever enjoyed a teammate this much before? The same fluttering happened in her chest again.

But maybe it was just the nerves.

Once everyone was gathered, her dad announced that it was time for both teams to present their meals. She and Connor presented their sweet and sour turkey over riced cauliflower, the "vegetable" side in the form of a mini pumpkin pie, and the Reese's and Lay's treats for dessert.

And then Jack and Noelle presented their grilled and sliced hotdogs smothered in a root beer reduction glaze with a touch of honey mustard, served on a bed of quinoa, with radish garnishes cut to look like flowers, a side salad of spaghetti noodles tossed with creamed corn and topped with crumbled pretzels, and the layered dessert in a glass. Which kind of still sounded gross, but looked pretty good, somehow smelled tasty enough, and was definitely impressive, given the ingredients she and Connor had bought for them to use.

As everyone sat down to try the foods, Katie pulled out her video camera to get everyone's reactions for the family Christmas Eve video.

After eating her fourth bite— surprisingly— of the glazed hot dogs and quinoa, she leaned closer to Connor and said, "Theirs wasn't nearly as bad as I thought it would be. And judging by the fact that you've finished yours, I'm guessing you felt the same."

Connor nodded. "And ours is better than I guessed it'd be."

"It's the sauce," Katie said, taking another bite. He should seriously submit the recipe to a cooking blog.

"I don't know," he said, picking up their dessert. "The Reese's / Lay's treats are pretty tasty. We made a good team."

As everyone finished eating, she managed to pull a couple of people to the side for interviews, like she did every year. Then they all gathered on the couches to watch the skits, and she filmed some more of everyone laughing and *aww*-ing.

Which was totally warranted, because her parents performed a skit about Christmas in space, with her dad wearing a colander as a helmet and her mom wearing slinkies on her arms like a space suit. They wandered a new planet to try to find a Christmas tree but ended up wrapping some flashing Christmas lights around a "space rock" that was really an upside-down bucket.

And then Julianne and her family pretended to be on a Christmas cooking show, with their seven-year-old as the host, the baby as the audience, and Julianne, her husband Ben, and her four-year-old all pretending they didn't realize they were using a collection of tools that would be more at home in a garage instead of the ones meant for a kitchen.

She filmed some more as Hope and her family presented their three-foot-tall Christmas tree decorated with a lollipop-theme, and Becca and her family presented theirs decorated with the aquamarine and navy blue of the Glaciers, complete with popsicle stick hockey sticks and hockey pucks made of chocolate Oreos as decorations.

Then they all voted on the winners, and she was looking through the video camera when her mom said, "And the trophy for *Best Dinner* goes to... Katie and Connor!"

She nearly dropped the camera. "We won?" She turned to Connor and shouted, "We won!" He picked her up and swung her in a circle with her fist held high in the air. When he set her back on the floor, she still felt like she was floating. And, well, connected to Connor in a way that she hadn't experienced with any previous

Santa Hat date. She wasn't going to let herself think about that, though. She gave Connor a high-ten, which was a medium-ten for him because the guy was seriously tall. "I can't believe we won!"

Her dad handed her the trophy, and she hugged it tight to her chest for a moment. Not only was their dinner edible, but they had won *Best Dinner*! Her curse was lifted. She passed the trophy to Connor so he could hold it, too.

He looked at the trophy, which had a wooden base with a slightly charred, very worn oven mitt, painted with gold spray-paint, and mounted on the base along with a very mismatched salt shaker and pepper shaker just in front of it. The front of the plaque read "Best Dinner." "*This* is the trophy we were competing for?"

"Hey, don't knock it. It has lots of history and stories and sentimental value."

"Do you have a special place on the mantle all picked out for it?"

"You know it."

As everyone was getting ready to leave and Connor was thanking her parents for inviting him, she noticed Becca's two oldest kids, nine-year-old Erika and seven-year-old Sadie carrying between them the Glacier-themed Christmas tree.

Once Connor finished talking to her parents, the girls approached him, and Erika said, "Our mom said that your hotel room is probably sad because it doesn't have any decorations, so we want you to take this Christmas tree with you so it'll be happy."

Connor immediately crouched down so that he'd be closer to the girls' heights, told them how much he loved the tree, how touched he was that they would let him take it with him, how amazing it was going to make his hotel room look, and how honored he felt to be able to put the tree in his room.

Her nieces were absolutely beaming. When Katie glanced at her sister and brother-in-law, she saw that they were, too. She looked back in time to see Connor stand again, checking out the details of the tree, looking like he genuinely appreciated it.

Was she being swept off her feet? Seeing hearts? Maybe a little. He had been pretty fantastic today. But anything could be faked for a day. Her feet were going to stay firmly planted on the ground and the hearts brushed away from her vision because she was determined to keep that skepticism in place for a little while longer.

six

CONNOR

IT SNOWED A BIT. The big storm hadn't come in yet— this was officially the "warm before the storm," and left just enough snow on the roads to really slow down traffic and make the drive between the arena to Mountain Springs that would normally take forty minutes take Connor nearly twice that long.

His nerves were getting more and more frayed the longer past one o'clock— the time he was supposed to arrive at Mountain Springs Elementary— that the clock climbed. This was his first town activity, and he was going to be late. He hated being late. And beyond that, he had some unexplainable need to impress Katie, and being late wasn't going to do it.

Okay, maybe it wasn't so inexplicable. At some point last night, he had to admit that he wasn't just enjoying the competition— he was enjoying Katie. He was attracted to her and wanted to impress her. All while not wanting to get involved with her, of course, since he'd be gone by the end of the season.

Because he'd been traded to the Glaciers so late in the Christmas season, many of the activities they probably would've asked him to participate in if he'd been there all month were past. He didn't know much about today's activity other than it was at the elementary school, which was fine. He liked kids.

He just wished he didn't have to go there today. It was a home game day, so most of the team started off the day with a workout before their mandatory team meeting, followed by a morning skate. This morning was only his second time practicing with his new team, and tonight would be his first game with them. He'd usually try to get a workout in after the morning skate, but had to skip today.

When he got into his rental car to head to Mountain Springs, most of his teammates were heading home for a pre-game nap because that was what they did to play their best. Outreach stuff like this usually only happened on non-game days. Adding it in today was hard, but with the short timeline they had to work with, it had to happen.

Whenever he wasn't focused on how slow traffic was moving, he was thinking about tonight's match-up, and thinking about plays— the ones he used on his own team and the new ones that he would be using with the Glaciers. He had excited nerves before every game, but it was different this time. He didn't have any past experience with being traded— he'd been with the Thunderstorm since he'd been drafted. It was strange to think that he'd be on the ice with a different team tonight. The Thunderstorm's rival, no less. He needed to be getting his head in the game.

No, he needed to get his head on this town activity.

"Oh, good, you're here," said the anxious woman with brown hair cut into a bob and an ID badge on a lanyard that read Ms. Messina when he finally made it to the school's front office. She didn't even have him sign the *Visitors Sign Here* clipboard on the counter— she just ushered him into the hall and said, "Let's get you to the stage quickly."

"Uh, the stage?"

"Oh, don't worry— we aren't having you perform or anything like that. That's just where we've got your costume. And my, you're a rather big guy. We didn't know which player we were getting until yesterday so we had to guess on the size, and hopefully we guessed right."

On the way down the hall, with her short heels clacking twice for every one step he took, she explained that the students had been collecting donations for a toy drive and that the older three grades were already in the gym, wrapping them. "You brought your jersey, right? Good, you can wear it while you're with the older kids."

For the younger kids, she informed him that he was going to be listening to their Christmas wishes. While dressed like Santa's elf, so he could relay the information to Santa.

"Oh, and expect the kids to be a little... rowdier than normal today. It's the end of the day on the last full day of school before Christmas break. You know how that gets." No, no he didn't. Not unless she counted the time when he was a third, fourth, or fifth grader himself. She led him to a storage closet on the stage where he could change out of his suit and into his jersey while she left to check on something with the younger grades.

Once he changed, he went down some stairs at the side of the stage, opened the door leading to the gym, and was immediately hit with a wall of noise and chaos. The stands at the game tonight weren't likely to be this loud. Luckily, his eyes quickly fell on Katie, who already had her camera up, filming, and he smiled in relief. It was incredible how much of the stress from the day melted away simply by seeing her.

Then she put the camera down and came over to him. Her smile seemed a little hesitant, like it had been a huge problem that he wasn't on time or because she was worried he wasn't up to today's task.

"It looks and sounds more chaotic than it is. That's just the sound of so many kids talking at the same time in a room where every sound echoes. For the most part, they're wrapping presents, like they should. They told me they want you to just grab a gift from one of those bins, find a spot at one of the tables, and wrap it while chatting with the kids around you. Then grab another present and find a spot at a different table. Easy enough?"

He nodded.

She studied him for a moment before asking, "Are you doing okay?"

He nodded again. "Great." Being here was practically the same as being back at his hotel, curled up in his bed for an energizing nap before a big game.

Katie put a hand on his forearm, a touch he swore he felt through his whole body. His eyes went to her hand first, then to her eyes. Once their eyes met, she said, "You've got this." She lifted the camera and started filming again.

Connor could go blade-to-blade with any player on the ice. So, he could wrap a simple present with a bunch of 8-11-year-olds. He grabbed one— a craft kit that looked like an easy box to wrap— and then went to a table where a group of boys who looked like they were probably fifth graders were waving him over. He introduced himself, and things seemed like they were going okay.

Until about thirty seconds in. He'd barely gotten the wrapping paper cut before one of the boys said, "My older brother's favorite hockey team is the Thunderstorm."

That... he wasn't expecting. Especially this far from Charlotte. He smiled. "They're a great team."

"Yeah. He says you're a traitor."

He might have been able to salvage the conversation at that point, but before he could, another boy said, "My uncle said he went to high school with you and that you've basically been a traitor your entire life."

The comments went downhill from there. And Katie was not only witnessing them all but getting them— and his reactions to them— on video.

The moment he was done wrapping the craft kit, he quickly left that table, put it in the bin for wrapped gifts, and grabbed a new one from an unwrapped bin. He decided to go to a table with a completely different demographic: third-grade girls.

They seemed a lot happier about having him join their table. In fact, the girl to his right really wanted to help him put the tape on his present. As the group chatted about books and gymnastics classes and gossip and what games they were going to play at recess and what presents they thought they were getting, he worked on wrapping presents. The girl next to him sometimes put the tape where she should, but more often tried to tape his fingers to the present, making everyone laugh when she did.

Then, when he turned his attention to a girl on his left who was talking about her brother, the girl on his right started placing the pieces of tape right onto his arms.

"He looooves hockey."

"Oh, yeah?"

"Yeah. He's twelve. He plays right wing, too. He thinks he's pretty good, but he doesn't get nearly as many assists as you do." Then her eyes shifted to the tape on his arm and she said, "Hey, Shaylie, that's mean!"

Then she, along with the girl across the table from him, both leaned in to help pull the tape off, and pretty soon, he had four hands pulling tape— along with all the arm hairs they were stuck to— from his arms.

He couldn't guarantee what expression was on his face, but he didn't yelp. He didn't curse. He didn't say any bad words. That had to be worth something.

The third group he visited didn't seem interested in hockey at all and only talked about Minecraft. He tried to join in their conversations, but he didn't speak the lingo. He didn't know what piglins and griefing and spleen meant, or what an Enderman, a creeper, or skelly was. The more he tried to join in, the more they looked at him like he was just another out-of-touch adult in their world.

What was he even doing there? Not anything good or helpful at all. He should be at his hotel in Denver, preparing for his first game day with the Glaciers.

He should have been glad when the teachers finally had the students line up to head back to their class-rooms, except that meant that it was time for Ms. Messina to lead him back to the storage room on the stage where there was now an elf costume hanging from a hook, waiting for him.

An elf costume that was much too small. He came out of the room wearing green pants that were super tight and about eight inches too short, pointy-toed slippers that slid on over his own shoes— barely— and a green button-up shirt with a red zig-zag collar that would only button up if he sucked in and then didn't breathe. The sleeves only came halfway between his elbow and wrists. Luckily, he'd been wearing a white t-shirt underneath his jersey, because if he didn't have it to wear under the elf costume, he'd be showing a good three inches of his stomach.

He opened the door to see Katie waiting, and she immediately tried to stifle a laugh.

"Katie, what do I do? I can't wear this." She brought her video camera up to film, which just annoyed him. "Seriously, what do I do?"

"Maybe I can check with some teachers, and see if any of them have a green cardigan or something stretchy that you can wear over it."

"Or I can just change back into my jersey. Tell the kids that Santa lets hockey players act as elves, too. Maybe make up something about us spending so much time on the ice as the reason."

But before he could even take a step back toward the room, Ms. Messina appeared and said, "Oh, my, that really doesn't fit. Well, there's nothing we can do about it now— the first class of Kindergartners is already here, and they are extra squirrelly today. Come quickly. We've got a throne ready for you to sit on and everything."

She led him to the front of the stage where there was indeed a throne. Maybe one they'd used for a school play. Katie had positioned herself on the other side of the kids, ready to film their interactions. She gave him a thumbs up with the hand not holding the camera along with a smile, which looked more like a grimace.

He couldn't take a deep breath, not in this shirt, but he took a shallow breath and then greeted the kids and told them he was one of Santa's elves and that he would let Santa know about their Christmas wishes. Ms. Messina placed the first kid on his lap, a five-year-old girl who kept poking at his shirt that was showing in the spaces between each button as she told him her mile-long list.

When she hopped down, Ms. Messina didn't place the next kid on his lap. The little boy just walked right up to him. So he reached down to pick the boy up, and as he was lifting him, the seams on both of his sleeves tore open at both the front and back, leaving only a few threads at the top and bottom to hold it on.

"Oh, my!" Ms. Messina said. "Um, children, it looks like Santa's elf has been eating his vegetables and has grown big and strong. We need to take a short break while we get a new shirt for him."

Connor breathed a small breath of relief— he hadn't popped any buttons, so a huge breath of relief wasn't exactly possible— and set the boy on the ground as he stood. The motion made one of the sleeves fall completely off, though, and it fell to the floor. Without thinking through the likely consequences first, he bent to pick it up, completely tearing the seam in the rear of his pants from top to bottom. And because they were so tight, he hadn't put a pair of shorts or pants on underneath them.

The entire class of Kindergartners immediately burst into stomach-clenching laughter. He had been booed at enough stadiums in locations away from home before, but even that wasn't exactly like a bunch of Kindergartners laughing because they could see your underwear.

Nor was it like having a vice principal who was probably old enough to be your mom take off her cardigan and tie it around your waist to hide said underwear and usher you off stage as your second sleeve threatens to burst free at the slightest move.

Or to have the woman you felt like you really connected with and are attracted to strongly enough to maybe forget your rules filming all of it.

WHEN CONNOR finally got back to his hotel, he didn't have long before he needed to leave to head to the arena. The front desk stopped him, though, and gave him a package that had arrived. He looked at the label and saw it was from his sister— it was the package she had put together the day he'd gotten traded and mailed to him. He took the elevator up to his room and opened it as soon as he walked inside. Items from home was just what he needed after the debacle at the school.

He smiled when he saw that his favorite cinnamon caramel hot chocolate mix was right on top, even after telling his sister that he didn't need her to send it. The contact lenses were a huge relief to find. He'd been wearing the same daily lenses for three days, and his eyes were dying for some new ones. Same with the socks. One of the t-shirts she sent was a greenish color, which would've been a life saver today.

The charging cords were a relief to find, too. He'd

been relying on charging his phone during practices by borrowing from other players. He laughed when he saw his pajama pants, though, and picked up his phone to call his sister.

The moment she answered, he said, "Really? The pajamas with the flamingo hockey players are my favorites?"

"Well, yeah. They're from your favorite sister."

"I should've seen that one coming."

"You really should have. I shipped off a bigger box of your stuff— you'll get it in a couple of days."

"Thank you. For both. And thank you for the hot chocolate mix. It's been a rough day, and it was a nice thing to find."

"Okay, hot chocolate doesn't usually warrant that much gratitude in your voice. I've got a few minutes before my next meeting. What happened today?"

He told her the entire frustrating and embarrassing story, from showing up late, to Katie being there to film everything, to the vice principal tying her cardigan around his waist. Not just handing it to him— actually tying it on.

"I've had two embarrassing experiences related to underwear since I got here, and Katie was there for both of them."

"Well, at least it wasn't the fifth-grade boys who witnessed this one."

He laughed. "True."

Now he needed to apologize to Katie for his frustration at the elementary school that probably ruined every bit of footage she filmed when he had just apologized yesterday for his behavior at the school dance. She was going to start thinking this was normal for him— act poorly, apologize, repeat.

He was quiet for a minute, and so was Laura. Then she said, "You miss home." It wasn't a question, just a simple statement.

"Is it stupid that I'm a twenty-six-year-old man— almost twenty-seven— and I do?"

"No. Missing the place that you love, the people you love, and the team you love has nothing to do with age and everything to do with the strength of your connections."

It also didn't help that Charlotte had been where his family moved to get a fresh start. That was where he'd flourished after everything had hit rock bottom. Maybe if he had gotten traded to anywhere other than the place where his dad had left their family, at the same time of year as when he'd left— the place where he'd actually hit rock bottom, things would be different.

"Hey, sis. I've only got about ten minutes before I have to change and head to the arena, and I'm not in the right head space to go play my first game with the Glaciers. I need you to pump me up."

"Okay," she said, and he could hear the squeak of her office chair as he was sure she was leaning all the way back, putting her feet up on her desk. "Tell me about the ice."

"The ice?"

"Yep. Talk me through what it's like the moment you first step a skate onto the ice. Don't think about where the ice is, just that you're on it. How do you feel?"

He closed his eyes and pictured it. The stands could be completely full with a raucous crowd, but the moment he stepped on the ice, everything always seemed to quiet. Knowing that his sister might razz him about a lot of things but never would about this, he was willing to talk through it out loud.

"From the first step onto the ice, I'm relaxed. But somehow energized, too. It's a feeling... I don't know. Like coming home. No matter where the ice is, the scent of the cold, the gleam on the ice, the expanse of white spread out before me always feels *right*. Like I'm in control of the space and even of time.

"That first glide is almost... sacred. Untouched by chaos. Smooth. The sound of the blade slicing across it is like music. It's a whisper, but so full of possibilities and potential. And gliding forward on it is powerful. Like *I'm* powerful. As I pick up speed and then make a tight turn, the centrifugal force pulling at me, it's like there's a trust, an agreement between gravity, the ice, and me. When I come to a stop, the side of my blade cutting across the ice, sending a spray of white ice in an arc, it reminds me that we're all working together to make something beautiful.

"The ice is where I'm most alive. Most myself. Most free. And as the crowds come back into focus, they energize and exhilarate me. They give me fuel to work with the ice, the gravity, and my team to pull off something amazing."

As I talk while picturing it, a calmness seeps into me. It gets me into the head space that I need to be in before a game. It grounds me and gives me energy I know I didn't possess when I first walked into this room.

Laura is quiet for a moment before she whispers, "Wow. Keep talking like that and I might become a hockey player."

He chuckled.

"Ice in a rink in Denver is the same as ice in a rink in Charlotte. Focus on your love of the ice wherever it is, and I can tell you that you'll be just fine."

"Thanks, sis."

"You're welcome. Sean and I have a date tonight, so I won't be able to watch, but call me tomorrow and tell me how the game went?"

"Will do."

"Oh, and tell me about this videographer who has caught your eye."

"What? How?" he sputtered. He'd said one sentence to Laura about Katie. And he'd kept it neutral.

"You give away much more in the tone of your voice than you realize. Now, I helped you today, so tomorrow, you tell me all about her."

seven

KATIE

KATIE WAITED for Connor in Mountain Springs' Downtown Park, standing right between a snow sculpture of an alien wearing a Santa hat while decorating a Christmas tree and a pirate ship with Santa as the captain. Connor wasn't late yet, but still, she wondered if he was going to show up after how things went yesterday.

Things at Mountain Springs Elementary School yesterday had been a disaster. The only genuine smile he had the entire time might have been the one he gave her when he first arrived and saw her. (Which was, admittedly, pretty fantastic and might have sent her heart a buzzing.) Yes, he also wore a smile when he went up to the first table to wrap a present with the fifth-grade boys — before they started smack-talking— but even that smile had seemed forced. Like he just hadn't wanted to be there.

She'd expected him to be good with the kids, especially because he had been so great with her nieces when they'd presented him with the Christmas tree to keep in his hotel room. An average response to her nieces would've been to thank them, tell them they did a great job, and then set the tree down. But he got down to their level, made them feel like they'd decorated the tree the best he'd seen in his life and that they'd given him the greatest gift ever.

Where had that Connor been yesterday? Yes, the boys had been rude. But he could've just joked with them about their comments instead of acting like they were being serious. Laughed with them about it. Pretended to be having a great time, even if he wasn't, so she could've at least turned off the audio and replaced it with something else.

As it was, she had no usable footage. The one part where he genuinely smiled at her? That shot had included no other people, and it was at an angle where it was impossible to tell that he was even in a school. She did try playing it in slow motion, though, just out of curiosity to see how it looked. His walk, complete with that smile, was amazing and looked epic. And, okay, she may have watched it through at least a dozen times.

Other than that, there really wasn't anything she

could send to the Glaciers. Her choice of footage would've been limited, anyway, because not all the parents had given permission for their child to be in the video, but she didn't have *any*. She'd spent the night tossing and turning and spent this morning wondering how she was ever going to pull off this job.

She hoped that yesterday was an anomaly. That he wasn't actually closer to being the kid who ruined the school dance back in high school than he was to being the guy she'd cooked a meal with at her parents' house two days ago.

But if nothing else, at least she validated her decision to not just go on initial impressions of a guy and to wait for more evidence to know if he was someone worth being interested in.

She shook out her gloved hands and stomped her feet in the snow a bit to get more circulation and warmth to them. And to help her nerves. Maybe she just needed to pull Connor aside often tonight and do what it took to get him in the right mindset so she could get some genuine smiles out of him.

Or... maybe not. From the moment she first spotted him walking toward her from a parking stall, there was a great smile on his face. When he glanced around the park, it didn't even fade. She didn't realize exactly how stressed she'd been until she felt relief at that smile. Maybe today wouldn't be the disaster that she feared.

When he reached her, she said, "So, I heard you won last night. Congratulations." It didn't explain yesterday, but maybe that was why he was smiling today. She pulled her camera from its case so she could get some footage of that smile in case it wore off.

"Thank you. It was a great game." He glanced again at all the snow sculptures lit by landscape lights before his eyes were back on her. "You're not a hockey fan?"

She looked at him, confused.

"You say you 'heard' we won."

Yeah, she "heard" it from the announcers. And from Emmalee's screaming. "Nah. I don't usually watch." Which was true, even if it wasn't true last night. She hadn't planned to watch, but then Emmalee brought home a bunch of flowers so she could watch on their TV in the living room while working. Katie had been at their table, attempting to edit the footage she'd shot during the day, trying to keep her attention off the game.

But she was curious. She had seen how Connor had acted at her family thing and had seen how he'd acted with the kids at the elementary school. Since the two glimpses she'd gotten of him didn't match up, she wondered which version she'd see at the game. That curiosity won out, so she brought her laptop to the couch to watch while she worked.

She couldn't really compare the Connor she saw on TV to either one. Although she did see the competitiveness that had come out during the cooking competition. And he did seem to truly love what he was doing when he was on the ice, even while in a fierce battle with another player over a puck. There weren't any interactions with kids, of course, so she had nothing at all to compare there.

"Hey, um," Connor said, rubbing the back of his neck, "I'd like to apologize for yesterday. It was a hard day for a lot of reasons." He looked like he wanted to say more but then changed his mind. But he added, "I imagine that made your job pretty tough."

She just blinked at him. He apologized *and* acknowledged the position it put her in? If she was keeping score, that would've earned him some extra points. And not that she'd give extra points for attractiveness, but his nose, which was now red from the cold night air, made his hazel eyes pop. And that 5 o'clock shadow along his jaw looked rather touchable.

"Thank you. Here's hoping tonight goes much more smoothly."

Like every night in the weeks leading up to Christmas, there were plenty of people in the park. Some were walking around, looking at the sculptures. Others were admiring the elaborate setup of Santa's village or riding the small train that circled the village. Some were looking at the life-sized nativity, and some were lined up at the hot chocolate gazebo.

Connor glanced at Santa's village and said, "Please tell me that I'm not here to put on an elf costume to help Santa."

Katie tried to hide a smile as she turned and started walking, Connor joining her. "I heard that the town's one and only costume was completely destroyed by a barbarian. No— we are going to that building just between the hot chocolate gazebo and the nativity."

"The community center? What's in there?"

How had she forgotten even for a moment that he used to live in Mountain Springs? He knew where everything was. It was his eyes. They distracted her. "All of the gingerbread houses that were submitted for the competition. *You* are going to judge them."

"Oh. I wish someone would've told me— my Gingerbread House Judging Certification has lapsed and I didn't get it renewed."

"I've heard the renewal process is a real bear," Katie said.

Connor nodded. "So many classes..."

"And so many terms to memorize..."

"And the certification test takes hours."

"And there's only so many hours in a day," Katie said.

"I feel like you really get me." He gave her a look that was part teasing, part something else. She wasn't sure what, just that it made her suddenly aware of her own heartbeat.

"Don't worry." Katie patted him on the shoulder. "That NHL jersey with your name on the back came with an honorary certificate."

"Whew!" He brushed the back of his hand across his forehead. "That's going to save me some embarrassment here in a minute."

Katie snuck a peek at him as they walked and smiled. She liked a guy who didn't take himself too seriously.

When they had almost reached the community center, a boy who looked like he was probably five years old came running up to Connor and said "Are you number seventeen?" It surprised her that Connor was already being recognized since he'd only been on the team for three days, but he was wearing a Glacier's coat, so maybe that helped.

Connor stopped and gave all his attention to the little boy, who was dressed in a puffy coat, gloves, and a knit hat with a big pom on top. "I am."

Katie immediately pulled her video camera out, just in case. She held it up just a bit, wordlessly asking the boy's mom for permission to get the exchange on video, and the mom nodded quickly, her focus going back to her young son. She started filming from behind the child, so she was getting Connor's face and not the kid's, but the more the little boy talked, the more she moved to his side so she could get all his animated expressions and gestures.

"I watched you last night and you did awesome! 'Specially that one part where you got that pass and took the puck down the side going *swish, swish, swish* back and forth, and that defender was right on you, so you turned around backward! *Swish, swish* with the puck, and he couldn't keep up and went *down*! And his skate nearly took out you, too, but no. You just turned around and *swoosh*!" He threw his arms up into the air. "Right into the net! It was so awesome! And the crowd was screaming so loud. We were only watching it on TV, but I'm pretty sure that we were screaming louder."

The boy's arm motions as he told about the play and his excitement were pure gold. So were the expressions crossing Connor's face as the boy talked. And all the Christmas festivities in the park were the perfect backdrop. She couldn't have planned a better composition for the shot.

"Wow— you really know a lot about hockey. Do you think you'll want to play?"

The boy puffed out his chest. "I already do."

"I bet you're pretty good at it."

As they talked, Katie noticed a second, much quieter boy who was holding back from the conversation a bit. He looked like he was about twelve years old, and if she had to guess, he was the animated boy's brother.

She was surprised at how quickly Connor noticed the boy and pulled him into the conversation. "Do you play, too?"

The boy immediately lit up and stepped forward. "I do. Right-wing, just like you."

She suddenly wondered if the boy was the older brother that the girl at the present wrapping station yesterday was referring to. If she was his sister, she didn't see her nearby, though.

Connor chatted with the two brothers, and when the older one asked for Connor's advice about what he should do if he wanted to play in the NHL someday, Connor gave it. He told him to focus on the fundamentals, not get caught up in complaining, work hard, and get the best grades possible. Yes, as a way to get into a college where he had a better chance of being drafted, but also because hockey was about a lot more than skill on the ice, and getting good grades helped prepare for all of that. Katie was pretty impressed by his answer. When she glanced at the boys' mom, she saw the woman was not only impressed, but grateful nearly to the point of tears.

This was the Connor she'd hoped she'd find for her videos. *And this is the kind of man I had hoped to find for me*, a voice in her head whispered.

I am working! she hissed back to the voice. But it

didn't stop the fluttering that was going on in her heart and the buzzing in her mind.

The boys sounded like they were finishing up, so she quickly asked their mom if she could call her about using the footage.

As she and Connor neared the community center building, she said, "You're really good with kids."

"You said that with an awfully straight face for someone who saw me in all my frustrated glory yesterday."

Katie lifted a shoulder in a shrug. "This feels more authentically you than yesterday did."

Connor studied her for a moment, but she couldn't read the expression on his face before he opened the door and they walked inside. The mayor and his eleven-year-old daughter, Breanna, were waiting to greet them and walked them to the room with the gingerbread houses. He explained that one of the tables had entries from elementary school-aged kids, one from middle school, one from high school, and two tables contained entries from adults. Connor needed to pick a winner from each age group.

Without even getting closer, an obvious winner from each table stood out as being way more impressive than the others. If he wanted to, Connor could've pointed out those four, been done in thirty seconds, and headed back toward his hotel in Denver moments later. She could kind of picture the Connor from the school yesterday doing exactly that.

But he didn't. He listened as the mayor explained Mountain Springs' tradition and how hard everyone worked. The mayor gave him a stack of cards that he could write on if he wanted to take notes on an entry to refer back to.

Connor looked down at the cards. "And what happens to these after?"

"We typically give them to the person who created that gingerbread house."

Connor tapped them against his hand a couple of times. "How long do I have to judge them?"

"We announce the winners at eight-thirty, but the doors open for people to come in and look at them at eight. So..." he looked down at his watch, "you have about thirty-seven minutes."

"And how many entries are there?"

"Forty-one."

Connor looked up at the ceiling for a moment. "Okay, so about forty-five seconds each, and that still should give us a few minutes at the end." He pulled out his phone and went into something. Then he turned to the mayor's daughter, who had been looking kind of bored but was trying valiantly to patiently wait for her dad, and held his phone out to her. "Do you mind being my timer?"

"Sure!"

"Okay, when I get to the first gingerbread house, push this button. When the timer goes off, say 'Next!' and press the *repeat* button. It's up to you to keep me on track to get through all of them. Are you up for it?"

"I sure am."

The moment Connor got to the first one, Breanna pressed the timer, and he spent a few seconds studying it, then he wrote the entry number on the card and started writing something about the gingerbread house. When Breanna said, "Next!" he moved on to the next one and did the same thing. Was he really going to write a note about the gingerbread house to every person who entered?

Yep. It looked like he was.

She'd thought she'd gotten a good sense of who Connor was that night at her parents', but everything at the school made her question it. Was this who the man really was? He did seem at home, natural, outside with the kids just a few minutes ago and now as he wrote on each card, where he hadn't at all yesterday at the elementary school.

She got some good footage of the houses in focus in the foreground with Connor blurred in the background and plenty with the focus on Connor as he studied the gingerbread houses, noticing details, and writing on cards.

A few times as she was filming, he looked right at her and smiled, and she wasn't entirely sure if it was a smile meant for the camera or for her. It wasn't just a happy smile or an "I'm enjoying helping out in this community" smile. If she read it right, it was an "I like you and I'm glad you're here" smile. Maybe even an "I'm attracted to you and really want those lips of yours on mine" smile.

But she could be imagining it. She would definitely be spending time rewatching some footage tonight.

When he had finished the final one, the mayor said, "Well, did you decide which ones are the winners?"

"I guess. There are four that definitely could be called 'the best.' But look at this one over here. It arguably isn't 'better' than that one, but look at all the details they put in. All the creativity. And check out the backside— there's a ladder leaning against the house, with the string of lights hanging off, like they weren't quite finished yet. And look at this one over here. Same thing— so much uniqueness and so many fun details. This one, too. There's a second one in each category that also deserves recognition."

Katie owned a business in a creative field. She worked part-time for her roommate in a creative field. Watching Connor notice creative details and appreciate them was doing things to her heart that she couldn't explain. Maybe because she'd never quite had it do that.

All she knew was that she was glad she had the camera rolling at this moment because she would definitely be watching it over and over.

And when he offered to personally donate prizes so that a second "Creativity Award" could be given to the entries that were clearly showing it in abundance, the buzzing in her heart and the buzzing in her mind seemed to click into sync.

eight

CONNOR

MOST OF THE gingerbread houses had been picked up by their owners, leaving only a handful behind. Except for the tables and half a dozen folding chairs that were placed randomly throughout the space, he and Katie were all that was in the room. Yet, Connor wasn't ready to leave.

He probably could've left as soon as he was done judging, but he'd had fun hanging out with all the people from town who came to look at the gingerbread houses before the winners were announced. He loved seeing them notice the same details that he had noticed when judging them and seeing if their reactions had been the same as his. He chatted with them quite a bit, too. And it was a lot of fun to help the mayor hand out the awards to the winners.

The whole time, he hadn't thought about the fact that he was back in Mountain Springs, about his dad, or even about hockey. And he *always* thought about hockey. Everything tonight had just been about being in that moment. It had been a long time since something had captivated him so fully. Since some*one* had captivated him so fully.

Instead of walking out to his car, as he should have, he walked over and sat down in one of two chairs close together and stretched his legs out in front of him. It only took a moment before Katie sat down next to him. Possibly because she felt like she couldn't leave until he did, but he hoped it was because she wasn't quite ready to leave, either. He was so drawn to her, and he hoped that she was having a hard time walking away from him, too.

"So," Katie said, "it looks like that honorary gingerbread judging certificate really kicked in."

"It definitely came in handy. Would you have chosen the same winners?"

"Oh, I'm not here to judge. I'm just here to document it all for the masses."

He nodded toward the video camera still in her hands. "What got you into videography?"

She shrugged. "I noticed that when you are in the middle of experiencing a memorable moment, it can be too much to take in all at once, you know? Like if you're dribbling a ball down the court and making a game-winning basket, your focus at the time is on the other players, the ball in your hands, the basket. It can't be on everything else, too, so you don't experience the moment all the way. If you're at a family Christmas party and are focusing on your ninety-eight-year-old grandma's delighted face when the tree is lit up for the first time, you probably aren't noticing the look of wonder on your nephew's face.

"But if you also have it on video, you can experience other parts of it later. Just like if you re-watch a TV show or movie, you catch different things the second time through. And re-watching lets you relive those same emotions you enjoyed the first time around. I like being a part of that."

"I have never thought of it that way."

"I started doing it to catch those moments for people, and by doing it, I kind of found out that I'm good at capturing the emotion of the event. Of knowing what to focus on."

Connor studied her, wondering if her camera would catch the sense of wonder on his face that he was feeling just by talking with her. He had known since that moment when she said they were on the same team in her parents' kitchen that he liked being around her. The more he learned about her, the more he realized why. He liked the way her mind worked.

He nodded at the few gingerbread houses that were left. "Did you ever enter a gingerbread house into this competition?"

"Oh, yeah. I was nothing if not up for a competition. Plus, we made them together as a family every year." She chuckled. "I was probably six the first year I entered one. I was always pretty independent, so even though I didn't exactly have the skill to make a gingerbread house without help, I was adamant that I do it myself. Of course, the walls kept falling down before I could even get a third one attached because I was working with two little hands and not a lot of patience or coordination.

"Eventually, I got one of those square boxes of tissues from the counter and just glued the walls to the side of that with the icing. But I'd had so many struggles leading up to it that the gingerbread was covered in icing smears and fingerprints, so it wasn't the prettiest thing ever."

Connor chuckled, too, as he imagined it.

"The roof was a different story, though, because I couldn't glue it to the tissue box. It was the most askew roof ever. I came across a picture of it a couple of years ago and was surprised that it somehow stayed put. Anyway, I finished, decorated it, and since I didn't think to empty the box of its tissues before commandeering it, I reached with my little fingers in between the roof pieces and tugged a tissue halfway out, and said it was the smoke from the chimney."

Now, he was fully laughing. "That's genius."

"It didn't win, of course, but I was so proud of that house!"

"As you should be."

"Did you ever enter a gingerbread house?"

Connor shook his head. "If we lived here when I was in elementary school, I totally would have. We used to make them together as a family, too. I always tried to see how creative I could get— building it unconventionally, using candies in less obvious ways, and putting in lots of details. I loved it. But we didn't move here until the middle of my freshman year. And by then..."

Katie nodded. "Things just get so much busier once you hit high school."

"Yep. It gets a little crazy. Besides, my family wasn't really doing family things by then."

That last part was something he wouldn't normally share. With anyone. Yet, it had just come out. And when Katie responded with an "Oh?" that was clearly an invitation to share more, he didn't change the topic like he normally would have. He realized that he felt not only comfortable enough around Katie to share, but felt like he could trust whatever response she'd have to it.

He took a deep breath. "I think maybe my parents decided we should move to Mountain Springs as kind of a last-ditch effort to save their marriage. Spoiler alert: it didn't work. I think that they wanted to get away from everything that was making them so busy in the city and move somewhere that had more of a community feel. Like maybe a change was what they needed to start over.

"But it didn't really fix anything. My parents were still there for me and my sister, Laura, but just not at the same time as each other anymore. Then they decided they were going to get divorced, and my dad gave us the speech about how he was still going to be there for us.

"I believed him. And at first, he was. He lived in Mountain Springs for the first little while, and we saw him all the time. Then he moved to Denver, and it got less frequent. He started loving that newfound freedom, I guess. It was harder to get him to come to things that were important to me or Laura. Then he just stopped coming around altogether.

"We'd been pretty close, too! He may have said it didn't have anything to do with me, but it was hard not to get your feelings hurt when he didn't seem to want to see you."

"I bet. I am so sorry you had to go through that." Katie reached over and placed her hand on his forearm, and it sent a tingling warmth radiating out from it. He just gazed at her hand for a few moments until she asked, "Is that why your family moved? I don't remember seeing you again after that dance."

He flinched. He did every time he even thought of the dance because it had been the culmination of everything bad. "It was. My mom knew something big needed to change for me. She literally let me throw a dart blindfolded at an NHL teams map and we moved to the one closest to where the dart landed. We started completely over there— everything we'd known was in Colorado."

"Wow," Katie said. "I can't imagine the bravery that required of your mom. Of all of you."

"And I love her forever for it."

"It was a good move? You didn't miss home?"

"It was exactly what I needed— I thrived there. It's coming back here that is hard." It wasn't a place he wanted to be. But he couldn't bring himself to tell her that he was going to request a trade.

"Well, I guess we need to change your memories here into good ones."

He smiled.

"You have an away game tomorrow, right?"

"Yeah. Minnesota."

"All right, on Friday, your third event to fulfill your contract is a hay ride. We'll make sure it's full of good memories."

nine

CONNOR

CONNOR STEPPED off the ice and headed down the hallway toward the visitor locker rooms after the game against the North Star in Minneapolis. It had been a hard-played game that left him frustrated and exhausted. They'd managed to squeak out a win in the end, but it wasn't pretty.

Normally, nothing except the game was on his mind for hours afterward. But he was barely off the ice and Katie popped into his mind. Yes, she'd been spending a lot of time in his head lately, but her coming into his mind right now was unprecedented for him. Maybe it was because he wanted to talk with her about the game. He loved every chance he got to talk to her— their conversations were easy and natural and made him feel like he could be himself.

Last night had been fun. Outreach was a big part of the NHL, and he didn't usually mind doing it at all. But it was tough having to do it while trying to gel with a new team, during Christmastime, and with such a tight window to fit everything in. But unlike the previous activity that had gone so disastrously, he'd really enjoyed every bit of last night.

And even more than the gingerbread judging, he enjoyed talking with Katie after. He always felt a strong connection with her whenever they talked, but last night, it had gotten stronger. After he spilled so much about his dad, they'd talked about random things, laughed, shared goals, and just chatted until the people closing up the building kicked them out. Then they got ice cream at an all-night convenience store and talked more.

And now, he really wanted to talk with her about the game. To work through what was going on. He had played hard— they all had, but things just weren't coming together with this team.

Although it wasn't super common, fights happened in the NHL. It was an intense game played by driven players, and sometimes emotions and frustrations spilled over. Sometimes it was during a game with a player on the opposing team. Sometimes during practice with a teammate. When you spent so many hours a day with the same guys over so many months, traveling together and rooming together, you could get on each other's nerves.

But fights with a teammate during a game rarely occurred. And it wasn't exactly what happened out on the ice tonight, but Briggs lifted his stick with both hands a few times like he wanted to cross-check Connor, and once looked like he'd much rather grab him by the jersey and give him a punch. That time was right after Connor had scored a goal, which made zero sense.

Connor missed the comradery he had with his old team. He couldn't get traded quickly enough.

He got the sense that if he talked with Katie about it, she would be level-headed and help him to see things more clearly. He liked the way he always felt after being with her, too, and had been all but counting down the time until he got to see her again.

But he shouldn't be wanting to talk more with her or to see her more. Not when he was doing what he could to be traded far from Denver.

Since they all still wore their gear, they mostly walked single-file from the ice to the locker room, and he had guys behind and in front of him. He heard the distinct muffled rhythmic clacking noise of walking with hockey skates on foam padding speed up right before Briggs knocked his shoulder into Connor's as he passed by him.

"Hey!" he called out to his teammate.

Henderson was just behind Connor and said, "Just ignore him."

"What is his deal tonight?"

"He's just agitated because we played the North Star, which is who Thompson got traded to at the same time as you. They were pretty good friends."

"It's not like I replaced him," Connor said, then used his teeth to undo the strap on one of his gloves. "Or that I had any say in it even if I had."

"I know. And he knows. He'll get over it."

After he showered and changed, he was at his locker when his phone rang. It was Vaughan— his old team captain and best friend on the Thunderstorm— so he stepped out into the hall to take the call.

"I caught the tail end of your game," Vaughan said through the line. "Sorry it was rough."

"Eh. It happens." Connor said, acting like it was no big deal when he was still very much feeling the full strength of the frustrating game, even if they did manage to pull a win out of it.

"I saw Briggs sizing you up like you are a Thunderstorm and the rivalry is still as strong."

"It was that evident, huh?"

"Pretty much."

"How's the new guy on your team?" He was the one whom Connor was traded for. He wanted only the best for the Thunderstorm, but a part of him didn't want the guy to be so amazing that they forgot about him.

"Let's just say that we're trying to not be like Briggs is to you."

"Oh?" He was pacing the hall as he talked, but he came to a stop.

"I mean, he's great on the ice, but he kind of sucks as a person. We've all been missing you over here."

"Believe me when I say that the feeling is very mutual."

"It was hard to see you go."

"I'm guessing it wasn't hard for the GM, but it's good to be missed."

"That's actually why I called. The GM pulled me in for a meeting after the trades went through to get the pulse of the team— thought you might like to know what he said."

Connor went back to meandering down the hall as they talked. "All right. Shoot."

"The Glaciers *really* wanted you. Apparently, they've been wanting you for quite a while, but the Thunderstorm didn't want to give you up."

"You're making that up."

"I swear on my grandmother's grave that it's true. But we needed a goalie— you know how badly we did— and we apparently had our eye on North Star's goalie, but they weren't willing to give him up. And Thompson is great. You know— you played against him tonight. Even scored against him.

"The Glaciers have a second goalie— the one you're using now— who is practically as good, so they went to the North Star and said they'd give them Thompson if the North Star would give us their goalie. Solving our biggest problem was a good move on the part of the Glaciers because it was the only way they could get us to give them you."

Suddenly, everything with Briggs made sense. Thompson was his goalie up until five days ago. And his friend. As a hockey player, it was your job to protect your goalie. In warmups, you never shot above your goalie's waist. But in a game, you were playing against the opposing team's goalie, and you got the puck in the net any way that you could. Thompson was unprotected, and Connor had shot high. And he scored.

Earlier in the game, the puck was in the crease, and Connor went into the crease after it and may have had some incidental contact with Thompson. He knew how much he hated it when the opposing team made contact with his goalie. Knowing that Briggs was still seeing Thompson as his teammate made his reactions understandable.

Connor stopped walking and leaned his back against the wall. "They gave up two players to get me?"

"Yep. Apparently, it took a while."

He didn't know if it made him feel better to know that he was wanted and that the trade wasn't as casual as it felt, or if it made him feel worse, knowing that there were four players who all got traded a week before Christmas.

After he and Vaughan hung up and Connor went back into the locker room, he decided that if he was being real with himself, he had to admit that maybe things hadn't been gelling between him and his new team because he hadn't been trying hard enough. All he'd been thinking about since he arrived in Denver was how to get back out. And if he played with that in mind, he couldn't play his best. And that wasn't the kind of player he was.

He needed to acknowledge that Erik Henderson had been a good friend and teammate since the first time Connor had met them, too. As they all headed out to the team bus that would take them to the airport and the plane back home, he decided that he was going to give everyone on this team his all. They deserved better than what he was giving them.

And as he made the decision, he wondered if he had come to the conclusion partly because of Katie. She didn't seem to ever be far from his thoughts lately, so maybe by deciding to give Denver a better chance, he was deciding to give the two of them a better chance, too.

KATIE

THINGS KATIE DID *YESTERDAY*: worked most of the day at Emmalee's flower shop, where they watched Christmas movies as they put together so many arrangements for people's Christmas tables.

Saw several ads from the Glaciers with footage that she knew came from other videographers, and then stressed about the fact that she didn't even have all of hers filmed yet and had sent in exactly zero clips so far.

Stopped by a shop in Mountain Springs to get a present for her brother-in-law, since she never got anything after Connor knocked into her at that department store in Denver.

Texted Connor several times about random things, including a picture she took of a life-size gingerbread man costume she saw at The Crafty One, suggesting that next year, he try it instead of an elf costume if he visits any schools.

Spent an hour editing the footage she'd gotten from the gingerbread house judging last night.

Spent way too much time replaying the parts where Connor talked about the creative details on the gingerbread houses that should be recognized and his advice to the five-year-old and twelve-year-old boys about hockey.

Went to the Waldrop home to film their big extended family Christmas party, where she caught their Aunt Martha accidentally setting her festive hat on fire with a candle, while their Uncle Bob dozed off and snored loudly into the microphone during karaoke.

Wondered how Connor was doing and how his flight was.

Looked up the score for his game. Several times. In between thinking about yesterday and how great it was to just chat with him for so long afterward.

Stayed up way too late editing more footage from the gingerbread house judging until she had something (but not everything) to send to the Glaciers, answered some emails, and worked on editing as much of her own family's Christmas video footage as she could.

Things Katie had done so far *today*: laid in bed, thinking about how tired she was and how she wished she hadn't stayed up so late last night. Although she wouldn't have changed anything about how many times she re-watched the parts where he smiled at the camera and she wasn't sure if it was an "I want to kiss you" smile or not. (She came to the conclusion... okay, *strong suspicion*, that it was, in fact, an "I want to kiss you" smile.)

And she thought about what she needed to do today — work a half day with Emmalee, edit a lot more footage, and then go on a hay ride with her family and one incredibly good-looking hockey player who also happened to be a great conversationalist.

The second she tossed off the covers and got out of bed, she wanted to get back in. Why was it so cold? Once in the hallway, she saw that Emmalee's bedroom door was open and she wasn't in there. Same with the bathroom. That was unusual. She walked toward the kitchen and living room area, where it only got colder.

As soon as she turned the corner to the living room, she saw an explosion of red, white, and yellow flowers and winter greenery. Flowers spilled out of boxes and containers, and greenery was spread across their coffee table and couch. Vases, pots, and containers were stacked up in the corner and in front of their TV. Rolls of satin ribbons, floral tape, and bags of cranberries were overflowing from a box onto the floor. Every available surface from their front door all the way through the living room and half of the kitchen table was swathed in blossoms and leaves.

Emmalee hurried over from where she'd been getting something out of the fridge. "I'm so sorry for taking up all the space! And sorry about it being so cold in here. All this really should be in a fridge, so I had to open the windows."

"Emmalee, what— " She noticed for the first time that Emmalee looked ready to walk out the door. She quickly looked at her watch— they weren't usually at work for another hour and a half— before she met her friend's eyes again. "How did this happen?"

"I know. I'm such a sucker. I said I wasn't going to take any more orders, but then a friend who's a florist in Nestled Hollow Facetimed me from the hospital. She's getting an emergency appendectomy, but she was supposed to do the flowers for a wedding tomorrow. She and the bride were desperate, so what was I supposed to do? They didn't have other options. So, I told her she could send everything here. I, uh, really wasn't expecting it to be quite this much."

Katie ran her hands through her hair and just kept them there, holding her hair away from her face, taking in the sheer mass of flowers— while trying not to shiver to death. "How are we going to do all this?"

Emmalee shook her head. "No, this is not on you. I am the one who said yes to this. You've got your own massive deadlines to worry about."

Yeah, this was Emmalee's problem, but Katie was her

employee *and* her roommate *and* her best friend. She had a responsibility to help her, so this felt like her task, too. "But seriously, Emmalee, how is this possibly going to get done by tomorrow?"

"I don't know. I'm going in to work now to get started on all the regular orders we still need to fulfill there. Plus, lots of people are going to be picking up orders all day. Then I'll have to find a way to do this after work and just... not sleep?" She grimaced. "Energy drinks for the win!"

"Okay," Katie said, "I'll hurry to get ready so I can start on it. Will I be more help working here or at the shop?"

"No, you can't. You have your own crazy deadlines today."

Katie shook her head. "I had already planned on working a half day. I'll help out for as long as I can." Maybe she could edit faster. Or stay up longer. Emmalee was going to need as many hours of her assistance as she could spare.

Emmalee let out a huge breath of relief. "You are a godsend. Working here would be better. I'll email you the list— it also has pictures of what the centerpieces and bridesmaid bouquets and boutonnieres and a few other things are supposed to look like." She pulled out her phone and forwarded Katie the email as she headed back into the kitchen, and Katie followed.

"I'll get right on it," Katie said as Emmalee sliced a bagel in half and started spreading cream cheese on it.

"Before I go, you have to tell me how things are going with Connor Greene. Was the gingerbread judging event any better?"

Katie leaned against the counter. "Last night was amazing. I even got that feeling of buzzing in my mind. You know the one where there's that excitement of possibilities and, I don't know, endorphins or whatever it is that makes you happy and hopeful and kind of swoony. I might have gotten some flutters with guys lately, but it's been so long since I've had the buzzing in my mind."

"Oh, wow— you're falling for him! I figured you'd get a crush because the guy seems super crush-worthy in every way, but wow!"

"I know. Is it crazy? I mean, I might only see him until the day after Christmas."

"Then you make sure to enjoy every moment of the next four days." She squealed, gave Katie a hands-free hug where she just squeezed with her arms since her hands each held half a bagel, and then said, "I've got to run. Call me with any questions, okay?"

And then she was out the door, *not* taking the cold with her, sadly.

Normally, Emmalee's advice to enjoy the next four days would be speaking Katie's language, because she was always up for dating someone who was going to make life more fun. But she wasn't sure she could be so casual with Connor. She'd been waiting for someone to come along who would just kind of grab her by the heart, and Connor felt like that someone. And when someone had your heart and just left, that leaving wasn't painless.

It took nearly an hour just to get everything organized and to figure out which flowers went with which arrangements, which bases to use, what ribbon, and to get it arranged in an accessible location. It took another thirty minutes to figure out how many flowers went in each centerpiece, boutonniere, corsage, and bridesmaid bouquet, and which ones to put aside for the floral swags.

It didn't help that the place was so crowded that she could barely move through the forest of flowers, or that she was wearing a coat, gloves, sweat pants, and a knit hat like she was outside in the winter. Which she practically was.

She was sitting at the table, working on one of the mothers' corsages when she got a text on her phone and leaned over to look at it.

Connor: What should I wear tonight?

She smiled and picked up her phone.

> Katie: Well, we'll be outside, so I would probably suggest wearing something warm over, say, flip-flops and swim trunks.

> Connor: Bummer, because I have new flip-flop socks I was hoping to show off. So, an outfit like this would be more appropriate?

Then he texted a selfie at an angle where it got most of his body, and she could see that he was wearing the hockey gear he must practice in, with the edge of the rink in the background.

> Katie: That's perfect. I'm a little unsure about the skates, though. Can you go up porch steps with those? I'd hate to see Glacier's prized new player break an ankle.

> Connor: True. We're going to be on actual hay, right? Maybe I'll ditch the skates and wear my farmer boots instead. I think they'll go pretty well with these padded pants and shin guards.

She sent the laughing emoji in response.

> Katie: So are you starting practice right now or just finishing?

Connor: Finishing, and about to head in to work out. Maybe get a massage.

Katie: Ahh. The life of a famous hockey star.

Connor: Yep. Nothing but massages, treatments, and food. Lots of food. What are you up to today?

Instead of responding with words, she sent a picture of the floral tornado surrounding her, making sure to get as much of it as possible in the picture.

Connor: Is that your apartment or the backstage of a flower show?

Katie: My apartment. Does it look cold? It's a giant fridge in here. My roommate owns a little flower shop on Main Street, and a floral emergency landed in her lap. I had plans to edit footage today, but until the hay ride tonight, I think this is all I'll be doing. She needs all the help I can give her.

Connor: Oof. Best of luck to you both.

A little over an hour later, as she was working on one of twenty— yes, twenty!— boutonnieres, a knock sounded at her door. She extricated herself from the mess of buds, greenery, floral tape, and ribbon that was on the table and her lap and went over to the door. She opened it to see Connor, holding a paper bag, smiling. She just blinked a few times, not registering how and why Connor was there, at her apartment.

"Hungry?" he asked, holding up the bag. "I brought lunch."

eleven

KATIE

KATIE DEFINITELY WAS HUNGRY— she had meant to get breakfast at some point but had been too focused on working. "What are you doing here?"

He stepped inside, closing the door behind him. His eyes widened as they scanned all the flowers in the room before they met hers again. "Well, after your stories about not wanting to accept help even when you need it, I figured that if I asked if you needed help with the flowers, you would say no."

She scratched her forehead. "Yeah, I totally would've said no."

"And you clearly could use help. I mean, I'm no expert, but this feels like a lot of flowers. So I figured I should just show up ready and willing to help."

"I don't even know what to say." She wasn't sure what to even think. It was hard to accept help, but this was help for Emmalee's thing, not hers, so it made it easier. And as much as she would've said no if Connor asked if she wanted help, she was so glad that he made the drive from Denver to Mountain Springs and showed up without asking. She *did* need his help. And it would be so much more fun with him there. "Thank you. Really."

"Anytime," he said as he walked over to the table, gently pushed some cuttings away from a couple of spots, and set the bag down. He gave a little involuntary shiver. "You're right— it does feel like a fridge in here."

"Wait. How did you know where I live?" Her eyebrows were creased in confusion yet she couldn't help but admire his strong face, the piercing blue eyes, the scar that ran along his jawline on the right.

"You said your roommate owned a little flower shop on Main Street, and there happens to be only one. So I went there, introduced myself, and asked for your address."

And, of course, Emmalee recognized him, because she would recognize any hockey player, and she was probably ecstatic to know that one would be helping with her business.

"Extra points to you for being so thoughtful and resourceful."

"Don't forget bonus points for bringing food."

"I never forget to award bonus points for food. How many, though, depends on what you brought."

"Sandwiches and soup from The Cozy Cabin."

"Are you serious?" Katie hurried to the bag, opened it, and did, indeed, smell the comforting goodness of The Cozy Cabin's butternut squash soup. She hadn't realized exactly how hungry she was until her stomach growled just knowing the delectable food was so close. "How did you know?"

"When we left the community center, you glanced over at the building. Your eyes widened just a bit and I heard a faint rumble from your stomach."

She just stared at Connor. "For real?"

Connor chuckled softly. "No. I asked your roommate what you would most appreciate, and then I went there and got it."

She smacked his shoulder playfully with the back of her hand. Then she pulled the items out of the bag. "Have you ever eaten at The Cozy Cabin before?"

He shook his head no.

"Oh, you're in for a treat. Sit."

As they ate lunch, Katie moaned a couple of times at just how good the food was. She might have been a little hungrier than she realized. But she was pretty sure she heard Connor moan a few times, too.

Katie told him about all that needed to be done— six

more boutonnieres, eight bridesmaid bouquets, and a dozen centerpieces, and that wasn't even counting all the pieces that Emmalee needed to do herself, like the floral swag and arches.

Once they finished eating, she taught Connor how to make a boutonniere, and they both started working on them. Katie couldn't help sneaking peeks at Connor. This tall, muscled man normally glided across the ice in padded gear, fending off other players as he hit a puck with a stick.

Today, he sat at her kitchen table, surrounded by flowers, holding small, delicate ones in his big hands, trying to gently hold them while intently wrapping floral tape around a small stem. If she didn't think that it would ruin the moment to pull out her video camera, she would've tried to capture it. Instead, she attempted to burn it into her memory because it might just be one of her favorite things she'd ever witnessed.

They had finished four of the six remaining boutonnieres when Connor said, "There is no way the two of us can do all those things you listed before we have to meet at your parents tonight. There's a guy on my new team, Erik Henderson, that I'd like to become better friends with. Do you mind if I text him to see if he's free to come help?"

The words "no way" sounded like a challenge. And

she was always up for a challenge. The words "more help" were something her very core wanted to say "no" to.

But this wasn't help for her; it was for Emmalee. There was only so much help that Katie could offer herself, and Emmalee was really never going to be able to go to bed tonight if she didn't have lots and lots of help. It might not even be possible for her to pull it off before the wedding tomorrow. Besides, she liked the idea of playing a small part in Connor making friends with a teammate. "That would be great."

When they finished the last of the boutonnieres and got the boxes of them moved to the kitchen counters, they worked side by side to clear the table of all the debris and get everything gathered for the centerpieces. She was just about to start explaining what they needed to do when there was another knock at the door.

This time, Connor was the one to answer it. And instead of a hockey player on the other side of the door, it was four of them. The one with sandy blond hair at the front, who Katie was pretty sure they called Henderson, said, "These loafers weren't doing anything productive, so I convinced them to come, too. Can we all help?"

Connor turned to her with an eyebrow raised in question and a grin on his face that made her suddenly wish she knew what he looked like as a ten-year-old.

"Of course! The more the merrier."

One of the guys gave an exaggerated shiver and said, "Feels like a hockey game in here."

A second added, "Except for the flowers."

"Nah," the first one said, "it just means we played well. Like when fans throw flowers on the ice after figure skaters do their thing."

It wasn't long before she had five— *five!*— NHL hockey players around the table in her little apartment. Katie filled the short but wide, clear, circular vases for the centerpieces with water, plant food, and cranberries. Then she set it on the table where she showed one player how to cut and place floral tape in a grid pattern over the opening to support the flowers they'd be putting in.

Three players, Connor included, were taking a stem at a time, removing extra and damaged leaves from the stems and any damaged petals from the buds, cutting the stem diagonally at the base, then placing them in a big bucket of water with flower food in the middle of the table.

The fifth player was preparing the spruce and eucalyptus stems for the base.

As they worked, Katie grabbed her phone and took a picture of the five of them hard at work and texted it to Emmalee along with the words *More help showed up.* Emmalee texted back a gif of someone screaming with unrestrained enthusiasm.

Emmalee: I'm closing the shop at four.
Sooner, if I can get the last person to
pick up their arrangement earlier.
Please, I beg of you, DO NOT LET
THEM LEAVE BEFORE I GET THERE.

When they finished the prep work, Katie gave them each a vase and moved the extras to the counter. Then she taught them how to make a centerpiece based on the picture that the florist sent. She started with the base of greenery— the spruce and eucalyptus— then added five focal flowers, which for this, were red and white amaryllis that were striped like a candy cane. Then she added the red roses and dahlias, giving tips on how to arrange them and when to cut the stems. She finished it off with some fern pieces and a few pine cones.

They watched with amazing focus. Was that an athlete thing? And then they all got to work. She took the moment to grab her video camera and started filming. They worked so intently that she wasn't sure they'd even noticed that she'd pulled out the camera.

A smile tugged at the corners of her mouth as she captured these five big, strong, athletic men who were known for their brute strength and relentless aggression on the ice as they hunched their broad shoulders over her kitchen table. They all had their brows furrowed in focus as they tended to delicate petals and stems with their big, calloused hands, choosing with great care where to place each one. These titans of the rink were doing such a gentle task. The sight of it was disarmingly charming. It was a dance of contrasts, and it was absolutely beautiful.

One of the players, a guy they called Calloway, placed his final amaryllis and said, "My mom would be so proud of me right now!"

Then one she was sure was named Bradshaw said, "Mine, too." Then he brought two fingers to his lips, kissed them, and held them high in the air. "Love you, Mama!"

Connor was the closest to him, and he glanced over and said, "Oh, did you lose your mom?"

Bradshaw shook his head. "No. She just told me when I was a kid that not only did she have eyes in the back of her head, but she had eyes in the back of *my* head, so I better make her proud whenever she wasn't around."

Henderson, the player that Connor had texted to come help, reached over and ruffled the back of the guy's hair. "Is that why you have this shaggy mullet? To cover the eyes?"

Bradshaw smoothed it back down. "You know it."

Katie was chuckling right along with them and trying very hard not to shake the camera as she did.

Davis studied his centerpiece, which was looking

pretty good, and said, "I think I'll take my little girl with me to get some flowers so we can make a centerpiece for Christmas dinner. My wife will be blown away."

It hit Katie that all these men were used to having cameras on them, so even once they did notice that she was filming, nothing changed. They continued to make jokes and rib each other over floral choices. The tough veneer of the hockey players seemed to melt away.

The more she filmed, the more she could tell that beneath everything, these were people with depth that went well beyond anything in the rink. They were brothers. They were friends. Even though Connor was new to the team, they had a shared experience as elite players who were at the top of their sport that bonded them even before they became teammates.

Since Connor was the player she was assigned to film, she spent a good amount of time zooming in on him, focusing on the way he bit his bottom lip when he concentrated. The way his left brow raised. The look on his face of... what was it? Focused contentment? The way he would put a flower stem in the vase and then look at it from the right and the left, adjusting it in small amounts before deciding that it was right.

After a good long moment of filming him, he looked straight at the camera— at her— and smiled. One side was raised just slightly more than the other, and he had a little sparkle of amusement in his eyes. His expression was mesmerizing. He picked up a flower by the stem and held it out toward the camera. She had been zoomed in enough that the auto-focus switched to the flower, bringing it momentarily into crisp clarity and blurring him, before she put the focus back on his face, blurring the flower.

That, combined with the expression on his face was perfection. She couldn't wait to pull this footage up on her laptop later.

She didn't know if the Glaciers could use footage like this, especially since it wasn't one of the scheduled events she was supposed to film and it included more teammates than just the player she was assigned to film. But this moment with five professional hockey players making floral arrangements felt like something that needed to be documented, regardless.

About the time they all finished their second center-piece, which meant that all twelve were finished, Emmalee came bursting through the door, like too many things had been keeping her back and she was finally free. As soon as she flicked the door shut with her foot, her hands flew to her face. "Oh, I don't think I've ever seen a more beautiful sight. Thank you so much for coming to help!"

She went around the table, looking at each arrange-ment, complimenting them on what a great job they did. Calloway pulled out his phone. "I'm putting this on social media!" He switched the camera into selfie mode and twisted it so he could get both his face and the floral arrangement in the shot. The other four did the same.

"The bride and the groom are huge hockey fans," Emmalee said. "They are absolutely going to go nuts for this! Can I tell them that you guys made them?" They all said yes, so she had them write their names and jersey numbers on a piece of floral tape that they stuck to the side of the vase so she could make a card to go with it on the tables tomorrow.

By the time Emmalee finished complimenting them, they all seemed more than ready to take on making a bridesmaid bouquet each. She suspected that it would give them additional bragging rights that they were all strangely excited to have.

At some point, she ordered pizza, and it showed up as they finished their bouquets. They all ate as they admired their work, bragged about their new skills, and smack-talked about whose was the best. Even though the temperatures in the room made the pizza go from perfectly warm to "fresh from the fridge" cold much too fast, the mood in the room was light. Fun. And something she wished could happen every day.

Especially the Connor part of it. As they all talked and laughed, his eyes kept finding hers, and he kept giving her that same smile. The one that told her that her heart was definitely in trouble.

After Emmalee thanked everyone profusely, Connor's teammates said goodbye, and Connor asked Katie if she wanted to ride over to her parents' for the hay ride in his car. Even though her head was telling her to pull back, her heart was saying "Grab every extra moment you can with this man!" So she told him yes.

As they walked out to his car, he said, "I'm really glad you let me come help today, even though you probably would've chosen to do it by yourself."

She definitely would've chosen to do it by herself, for sure, but she wouldn't have *preferred* it. "Today was fun. And the help lifted a huge weight from my shoulders."

He stopped walking and studied her before holding his hand out flat near the top of her head, squeezing one eye shut like he was trying to gauge her height. "I can tell. You're taller now than when I arrived."

She chuckled, then met his eyes. "Thank you for everything today." Her voice seemed to come out with all the sincerity she was feeling.

He held her gaze for a long moment. Long enough that something really sparked between them. And something was happening to her heart. She was falling hard. And then the man glanced at her lips and something happened to her stomach, too. And suddenly, all she could think of was kissing this man. Grabbing him by the coat and planting her lips on his.

But then he reached into his pocket, pulled out his keys, and pressed the button to unlock his car. Then he gave her that smile that was melting her just a bit more each time and opened her door. So she gave him a smile right back and got inside.

twelve

CONNOR

CONNOR WALKED with Katie onto her parents' front yard, which was not only covered in a layer of crunchy snow but was filled with decorations. In the midst of the decorations sat a couple of tables, and people in coats stood around, socializing. At a quick glance, it looked like everyone who was at the Santa Hat activity earlier in the week was present, plus a few extras.

"I'm sorry that I'm having you go from spending all day in a cold apartment to spending all evening in the cold outdoors."

"You do remember that I hang out on ice for a living?"

Katie laughed. "So I guess you're used to it."

"Yeah, don't worry about me."

"Still, we should get hot chocolate first."

As they neared the hot chocolate table, Katie sucked in a quick breath. "I did tell you that caroling is part of the hay ride, right?"

"No."

She grimaced. "Sorry about that. Can you sing?"

"*Well*? No. *Enthusiastically*? Yes. Mostly, I've learned that if you do anything enthusiastically, people will forgive it not being done well."

She smiled. She'd asked the universe for a man who would serenade her, even if he couldn't sing. It sounded like the universe answered. "You and my gran-gran would've gotten along well."

Mr. and Mrs. Allred were behind the table, ladling hot chocolate into cups. Connor shook Reid's hand and thanked both he and Elizabeth for inviting him, once again, into their family traditions. He also verified that it was still okay that he come to spend the three days he had off hockey for Christmas with them. The closer it got, the more grateful he was to have a place to go. Before long, he had a cinnamon caramel hot chocolate in his hand that was even better than the stuff that Laura had overnighted to him along with his essentials.

As another family walked toward them, Katie said, "I think you've met all of my family. And this is my brother-in-law Jack's sister, Rachel, and her husband, Nick. These are their kids Aiden and Holly. And this sweet little girl," she said, bending down to ruffle the fur at the sides of the neck of a rough collie that looked like she could be Lassie, "is Rosy."

"Oh, hey," Aiden said, "I saw you on TV!" He looked to his mom. "He was the one on TV, right?" Then he turned and called out louder, "Grandpa, is this guy on your team?"

"He sure is, buddy."

"Hi," Connor said, holding his hand out to the little boy. "I'm Connor Greene."

Aiden, who looked like he might be seven, grinned at him. "I liked watching you play. It made me want to play hockey, too."

Forget making it to the playoffs. Comments like that made him feel as though he had the best job in the world. "That makes me happy to hear."

The big black lab that he'd seen at Allred's home during the Santa Hat activity came over to Aiden, and Aiden started rubbing the sides of her neck. Then Katie asked, "How is Bailey doing?"

"She's doing so good," Holly said. "She had five of *the cutest* little puppies. I'm talking like the cutest puppies on the entire planet."

"They really are," Katie said to Connor. "I got to see them a few days ago." Then she pulled out her video camera. "I better start filming."

She shadowed him as he chatted with everyone for a

bit. The day was already long, but it had been a good one. He bonded with some of his teammates more this afternoon arranging flowers, of all things, than he had since he'd first stepped foot in Denver.

He felt like he'd bonded with Katie more, too. He never would've guessed he would've liked making floral centerpieces or bridesmaid bouquets, but he'd had fun doing something so out of the ordinary with her. He suspected he would have fun doing pretty much anything with her.

He could tell as they'd stood outside his car that she wanted to kiss him, and he really wanted to kiss her. He nearly did. But he really liked Katie. Possibly more so than anyone he'd ever dated. And he didn't want their first kiss to be right after she thanked him for his help as if he expected something in return. He didn't want it to feel like a "You're welcome"— he wanted it to be something much more than that.

They all made their way to the hay ride, which was two flatbed trailers hooked to Mr. Allred's truck. They both had hay bales stacked in ways that gave plenty of seating options on both trailers, with blankets covering them. As soon as he and Katie took a seat, Aiden said, "Okay, I'm sitting right here," and sat down next to him. Holly sat on Aiden's other side.

"Do you like hockey?" the boy asked.

"I do."

"Is it cold on the ice?"

"It is at first. But we dress warm, and once we start really playing, it kind of keeps us from getting too hot."

"That's cool. Do you like scoring goals?"

"It's my favorite part."

"Are you in love?"

"Wh— what?" Connor stammered.

"My uncle Jack fell in love on this hay ride two Christmases ago."

"Oh, yeah?"

"Uh, huh. And my mom fell in love—"

"—with my dad," Holly cut in.

"—last Christmas. Well, maybe they didn't fall in love on the hay ride there. Maybe it happened at Jack and Noelle's wedding because that's where the hay ride went last time."

"But they for sure fell in love on the hay ride back," Holly said. "Maybe *you* can fall in love this year."

"Wow. This sounds like a really magical hay ride."

Both kids nodded, then Aiden said, "It is."

He glanced at Katie, who looked like she was trying not to chuckle audibly, and gave her a smile, keenly aware that she had the video camera on the whole time and likely caught whatever reaction had been on his face.

He quickly got into the groove of the hay ride. They *ooh*ed and *ahh*ed at every house they went past that had lights and/or Christmas decorations in their yard. When Mr. Allred pulled over at someone's house, they all hopped off, including the dog, Captain, went up to the door, and started singing a Christmas carol. He made sure to sing enthusiastically. Mostly because it seemed to make Katie happy.

In between the stops, Katie filmed quite a bit, including several interviews with her family members for the video she was preparing for them. She even interviewed him. She filmed the caroling, too, which he was pretty sure was part of what she would send to the Glaciers.

Mr. Allred had driven them in a big loop through Mountain Springs, making a lot of stops for them to sing, including several houses where they were having big family parties. When they were a couple of blocks away from the Allred's home, Katie said, "I've been sitting too much and my legs are cold and getting numb. Do you want to walk the rest of the way back with me?"

Of course, he did. As Mr. Allred came to a stop at a sign, they hopped off the trailer, then gave him a wave, and he continued on without them.

A few stops back, snow had started to gently fall. It wasn't the bigger storm they were supposed to get— just a gentle snow before the storm. Enough to look beautiful as it lazily fell, making the night a little less dark and a lot more quiet.

"Thank you for being such a good sport about all this," she said. "I've had nightmares of being assigned a player who was a grump, and I ended up having no good footage to turn in."

"Oh, like our first filming session at the school?"

She chuckled. "Exactly like that."

"Did I ever apologize?"

"You apologized *and* acknowledged that it made things rough for me as the person under contract to turn in the footage. But you didn't apologize while dressed as Santa's elf, which would have made it even better."

"I'm pretty sure that costume is in the landfill now."

"Bummer," she said, her breath making little cloud puffs with her words. "What I wouldn't give to see a *smiling* Connor Greene wearing it."

Why did that make him want to go out and buy an elf costume?

There was only maybe half an inch of snow on the sidewalks and roads so far, but everything else still had several inches from a previous storm. The new snow softened everything. It reflected the light of the moon, making it feel almost like it glowed from a light within, casting everything in a faint, bluish light.

As they came under the warm golden glow of a street light, Katie stopped and looked up. The light caught each of the snowflakes, highlighting their meandering path to the ground. "It's so pretty!"

So was his view. She tilted her head up, opening her mouth to catch snowflakes on her tongue. She caught several and grinned, and he just gazed at her, bathed in the golden light, snow falling all around them. Those blue-with-gold eyes held the perfect mix of determination and optimism. Her knit cap was pulled down over her ears, and her light brown hair peeked out just enough to frame her face, showcasing cheeks and a nose reddened by the cold and a smile that could melt an entire rink of ice.

During the hockey season, he never kept his eye out for someone he might want to date. In the off-season, sure. He'd found plenty of people to go on dates with, but none who ever felt right. None who pulled at his heart the way Katie had from that first moment at her parents' home. Or really, since that moment he had knocked into her at the department store, making them both fall to the ground.

How, when he moved to the one place in the country that he least wanted to go, did he manage to find the one person who would capture him the way that Katie had?

A snowflake fell onto her eyebrow. He pulled off one of his gloves and reached out to brush it away with his knuckle. Another one fell on her eyelash and she blinked a few times, never taking her eyes off of his.

Until her eyes fell to his lips. They came immediately back to his eyes, searching. He moved a bit closer to her, a signal that if she wanted a kiss, he wanted it, too. With everything in him. She leaned in slowly at first, then she slid her arms around his neck and pulled him close, pressing her lips against his.

Her lips were cold from the night air, but as soft as the falling snow. They moved against his carefully as if she was testing for his reaction. He put his still gloved hand at the small of her back, pulling her close, his other hand sliding to the back of her neck, his fingers, still warm from being in a glove, tangling into her hair.

Her lips responded by moving more purposefully, more sure, as she pressed against him and the soft snow fell all around them. When she ended the kiss, she did by only pulling back the smallest amount, keeping her body still pressed against his, the warmth of her breath mingling with his, their cold noses touching.

"Oh, my," she said. "You, Connor Greene, are an amazing kisser."

He smiled into her lips, then gave her another kiss. "Feel free to make sure that's still true as many times as you'd like." He hoped she wanted to take him up on it often. It wasn't like he hadn't experienced some decent kisses in his life. But he was pretty sure this kiss just changed his world. Nothing was ever going to be the same.

thirteen

KATIE

SINCE KATIE, Connor, Connor's teammates, and Emmalee were able to get so many of the wedding floral arrangements done yesterday and after she got back last night, Emmalee was confident that she could get everything set up at the wedding today without Katie.

Which was good, because editing videos was a very time-consuming process, and Katie had so much work to do. She really needed to spend every second of the day doing it.

She was glad that it was work she enjoyed doing. She might even like the editing more than she enjoyed shooting the videos themselves. She got to see everything again when the emotions of the event weren't currently happening and gauge whether she was able to capture that same emotion in the video.

And if it wasn't quite there, by cutting out parts and placing other parts next to each other, she was able to pull that emotion through. Especially when she added just the right music. Editing was the part of the process when she could look at it most objectively.

What made it hard to be objective? When you kissed your subject the night before editing all of the video footage he was in. Especially when it was a kiss that took the bar she had set, flung it clear up into the clouds, and stayed there. She had never experienced anything like it and hadn't been able to stop thinking about it since.

Was it because Connor was just so much better at kissing than any other guy she'd dated? Or was it because he, as a person, was so much better? Because she had fallen for him so much more? Because he was exactly what she'd been waiting for all along?

Whatever it was, it meant that, as she edited, her eyes were drawn more to things like his lips. To how she could pause it at any moment and study the exact expression on his face, guessing just how he was feeling in the moment. She was working at her desk today, where she could connect her laptop to a much bigger monitor to have more space to move things as she edited. So she got to see him in crystal-clear, ultra-high-definition resolution on an expansive screen.

She'd bought the monitor earlier in the year to increase her productivity, but she couldn't exactly say it was helping her today. But stopping to smell the roses was an important thing to do, right? A healthy thing. That was basically what she was doing.

Her phone lit up with a picture of Connor's face that she'd taken just a couple of days ago, and it made her heart leap and get all giddy just at seeing it. She swiped to answer the call and put it on speakerphone so she could still work while they talked.

"Well, hello there. What are you up to?"

"Oh, just looking at the video of you smiling at the camera on repeat. You?"

He chuckled, and the sound made her smile ridiculously big.

"I am getting my suit on..." there was a slight pause before he continued, "because I need to be down at the team bus in about fifteen minutes to head over to the arena." A few of his words had sounded a little muffled and she was pretty sure it was because he had just taken off his t-shirt. And now she was imagining what that big, strong, athletic body of his looked like without a shirt.

To stop herself from letting those thoughts continue and distract her even more, she asked, "Are you required to always wear a suit to the arena?"

He had an away game today— against his old team, actually— so she'd spent the morning thinking about him as he was getting on the team bus to head to the airport. As the plane was in the sky. As he was landing and heading to the arena for a practice skate. The fact that he'd texted her several times during the day made it that much easier.

"Yep. On home game days, we wear a suit to the arena. When we get there, we change into our practice gear to skate. Then we change into workout clothes, exercise, shower, and change back into a suit. Then we leave and go get lunch or go home for a pre-game power nap and change out of the suit. Then we change back into the suit, go to the arena, change into our uniform, play, shower, change back into the suit, have media interviews, head home, and then change out of the suit again. At away games, it's not too different."

Katie couldn't help but laugh. "Wow, you're a pro hockey player *and* a pro clothing changer. I'm pretty sure that makes you a part-time fashion model."

Connor's laughter echoed through the phone. "Well, I do like to think I look pretty good strutting down the runway, also known as the arena corridor. But it does feel like we waste a lot of time just putting things on and taking them off. I'm still waiting for quick-change Velcro suits to be invented."

"Now *that* would be a fashion statement. They might ask you guys to make a calendar of you in your suits instead of in your team uniform."

"You do photography as well as videography, right? Maybe we could hire you to make us look good."

She gazed at his face in the video that was paused on her big screen. "Oh, believe me— you don't need my help to look good."

"I think I need to call you before every game to pump me up. You're quite good at it."

Katie grinned.

"We had a bit of a break before the game, and I got to see my mom, stepdad, and sister. They met me at the hotel we're staying at."

"Oh, that's fantastic!"

"Not the same as seeing them at Christmas, but still pretty great."

"Did your mom have a hard time saying goodbye?" She had heard Connor talk about his mom enough to know that she probably did.

"Yep. Since this was our last game before the break, she really wanted me to stay for Christmas instead of flying back with the team. She gets that the storm coming in will cause delays in Denver for days and would compromise my ability to get back for our home game on the twenty-seventh. And that I'm expected to make travel decisions that align with my professional commitments, but that doesn't make it easy."

"Well, it's Christmas, and you're her son. She has the right to be sad that you won't be there, even if she does support the reason why."

"She says she thinks she'll love you. If she just heard you say that, she'd be convinced of it."

Katie was grinning, just knowing that he told his family about her. Knowing that his mom liked her without even meeting her was icing on the cake.

"Are you going to watch my game?"

"I will be editing, but you better believe I'll have it playing beside me as I work."

"Then I'll give a little wave to you at faceoff."

"I'll be watching for it."

"I'll see you tomorrow?"

"Yep, tomorrow," she said, and they told each other goodbye. When she first found out that her dad had asked the guy who had spilled punch all over her dress at her first high school dance to spend his three-day Christmas break at their home, she hadn't been happy. Now, though, she was very grateful that her dad had that kind of foresight. She chuckled. He would probably say it was "a Christmas miracle!"

Things were going so well with Connor. So well, in fact, that doubts had started creeping in. Could something this good last? Since her dad not only knew way more about hockey than she did but also worked for the Glaciers and therefore often had inside information, she called him this morning. She had never been too interested in hockey, but since she'd grown up in her family, she'd heard a lot of things even if she hadn't been trying to.

So she knew that there was a trade deadline. Google told her that it was just before the playoffs and that a lot of teams traded players then. That was just a couple of months away. She had already fallen so deeply for this man and knew that with him, she had the potential to fall so much further than she'd ever fallen. She needed to know how much she should worry about him being traded away.

Her dad had confirmed that players were often traded at the deadline. "But sweetheart," he'd said, "they really wanted Connor and worked hard to get him. They aren't going to trade him away anytime soon." It had been a huge relief.

She got to the part of the footage where she'd had the camera on Connor while he and his teammates were arranging the centerpieces, and he'd looked straight at the camera.

At the time she'd shot the footage, she'd known it was something special. The expression of joy mixed with contentment on his face. The amusement in his eyes. The way one eyebrow raised just slightly. The smile quirked up more on one side. What that smile did to the little crease at the side of his lips. The unblemished amaryllis that he held out to the camera. The lighting had been perfect. The chill in the room had given his cheeks and nose a color reminiscent of his look while skating on the ice.

She paused the video and just took in his face. It was unmoving, yet still conveyed so much emotion. But it wasn't just that his emotions were recognizable on him — it was that his emotions could be felt, experienced, just by looking at him. It was mesmerizing. The longer she looked, the more depth of emotion came through. The more she felt everything.

She wanted to take the still frame image and blow it up large enough to cover an entire wall in her room. She wanted to wake up every morning to that face. To experience that sense of wonder and happiness that he exuded. To look into those beautiful eyes and feel that same bliss, comfort, and contentment.

It wasn't exactly the footage that the Glaciers had been asking for, but she was going to send it to them, and she hoped that they would show it. If they wanted fans to fall in love with their new player, this was going to do it. Yes, Connor was good-looking, and this was a shot that captured that, but they were going to fall in love because of what it made them feel. This image and this seven seconds of footage had the potential to go viral. If it did, it wouldn't just be Glaciers fans who would fall in love with him— the whole country would.

When she finished all of her edits of Connor and his teammates working with the flowers in her apartment, she had taken her thirty-two minutes of footage and gotten it down to three files to send to the Glaciers. A ninety-second version that included all five players, a two-minute version of just Connor, and the seven-second clip of him holding out the flower. All three videos captured the mood in the room as the big athletes tackled a delicate project that wasn't so common for them to tackle, experiencing joy and a sense of fulfillment doing it that maybe they hadn't expected to experience. It made them relatable. It showed their vulnerability. It captured their humanness.

It was, quite possibly, her best work.

She sent it off to the Glaciers, her chest buzzing with the thrill she always got when she created something, multiplied so many times by what it was that she created. That Connor was the focus of her creation.

She took a moment to stand and stretch, and then she got started on the hay ride footage. Once she finished that, she needed to edit her own family's video with the activities they'd done this season and the interviews with her family members— the one they'd watch tomorrow, on Christmas Eve. She'd have to work quickly to finish all of it in time and still go to bed at a decent hour.

And she had a hockey game to watch.

CONNOR

A STRONG MIX of emotions hit Connor as the Glacier's team bus pulled into the parking lot of the Thunderstorm stadium in North Carolina where he'd spent his career playing. Loss and longing, a bit of regret, some sadness and exclusion, happiness at the memories he'd made in this place. Plus so many things he felt intensely but couldn't begin to name. Counting back the days, he realized it had only been a week since he'd last been there. It was simultaneously as if no time had passed and that weeks had. Maybe even months.

It didn't help that all day long, the sports commentators had been donning their Santa hats and talking about this final game before the league's three-day Christmas break. They played up the rivalry between the Glaciers and the Thunderstorm and how the Thunderstorm's D-

Man, Ackerman, was very recently on the Glaciers' team and that the Glaciers' right wing was quite recently on the Thunderstorm's.

They kept talking about how Ackerman had been a big source of the rivalry between the two teams, especially after last year's playoffs and wondered how it would all turn out. Were the two of them going to go easier on their old teams? Harder? Make mistakes? Play their best to show their old teams what they gave up? Had they gotten a chance yet to bond with their new teammates? Was swapping players going to be like an olive branch to soften the rivalry between these teams? The only thing they could all agree on was that emotions were going to run high on the ice.

The commentators also talked about the fact that since Ackerman was on defense and Connor on offense, and that they played on the same side of the rink, they were going to be matching up a lot. They were no strangers to playing toe-to-toe against each other; they'd just never done it before with their jerseys swapped.

Connor wanted to call Katie and talk it all out with her. He knew she would keep a level head, bring out the best in the situation, keep him grounded and focused on the right things, and leave him pumped up and ready to take on the world. Not only would the guys razz him and his coach get after him for it, but it was Connor's job to ignore all the voices outside of his team and to get his head in the game.

So he did, even though the response of the fans toward him being back in town seemed to be a mix of support and resentfulness, leaving him feeling like he'd lost a sense of home and belonging. He got off the bus with his team, grabbed his gear, and headed inside. It felt strange to head to the visiting team lockers instead of the home team ones.

It was strange to put on a different team's jersey inside this particular arena.

It was strange to go onto the ice and warm up on the opposite half of the ice.

And it was strange lining up at center ice for the faceoff against his friends and very recent teammates.

He made eye contact with the Thunderstorm's new goalie. He gave the player a nod— an acknowledgment that they both got traded to new teams and had to move eight days before Christmas and that it was hard.

He found the camera, sent a little wave and a wink to Katie, and then turned his focus to the game.

It was clear from the moment the puck was dropped onto the ice that it was going to be a tough game. And it was clear from the moment Ackerman body-checked him into the boards— a short twenty-three seconds into the game— that his opponent was going to play hard and that the game would get physical. Any time Connor had the puck, Ackerman hit into him. It was all a legal but exhausting way to play.

As the game went on, Ackerman's hits became even harder and of the less legal variety, including a penalty for boarding, when he came from behind and hit Connor in the back, pushing his face into the boards when he didn't have the puck, slashing at his stick, and, in the third quarter, grabbing him by the jersey and punching him. They both spent time in the penalty box, but Ackerman got three times the number of minutes that Connor did.

Connor gave his all at every single game he played. But knowing that Katie was watching made him give more of himself than he thought he could. It was a hard-fought game from every single player on the ice— not just from Ackerman and Connor— from beginning to end. It was as if every one of them was looking to be at the top of the leaderboards on body checks. As hard as every one of them played, though, when the end-of-game horn sounded, the scoreboard showed the Glaciers down by a goal.

Connor and his teammates headed off the ice and toward their locker room. As soon as they were away from the view of the cameras and the fans, Calloway took off his helmet and chucked it down the hallway, letting out a string of swears. Connor got it. The loss felt personal.

Even still, he couldn't pass up the chance to see his old teammates off the ice once the meeting with the coaches to review the game was over. He headed toward the Thunderstorm's locker rooms, his body already aching from the beating it had taken. He was about to text Vaughan to see if he could meet him in the hall so he didn't have to risk a possible incident with Ackerman when he rounded a corner in the corridor and saw his friend walking toward him.

"Hey," Vaughan said. "I was just coming to find you." He and Vaughan greeted each other with a half-hand-shake, half-hug and chatted about the game for a few moments, just like they used to after games. It was bitter-sweet to talk to him in the same way they did when they saw each other daily, knowing they were going home to separate states tonight and he wouldn't see him again until their teams played each other again in April.

"I have an old teammate who plays for the Explorers now," Vaughan said, "and he told me there are rumors that they're looking to trade their right wing."

Connor's eyebrows raised.

"Ohio's only an hour-and-a-half flight from here, and they're a great team. You should consider talking to your agent about that possibility."

He imagined what that might be like all the way back to the locker room. It would be nice to be closer to home. But today only left him feeling pulled between conflicting desires. He missed Charlotte. He missed this stadium, this team, these fans. At the same time, though, he couldn't wait to get back to Colorado to see Katie again.

IT WAS LATE when the team's plane landed at Denver International, and even later by the time Connor finally got back to his hotel. He fell asleep quickly and didn't wake nearly as early— or as pain-free— as he had hoped. He had a bit of shopping he wanted to do before he headed to the Allreds' home to spend the next three days, though.

He stretched his shoulder muscles a bit to ease the soreness as he walked out of the store and into the snow, pulled out his phone, and called Katie. Last night's game had been a punishing one, and he was aching and sore all over.

"Good morning!"

It was so good to hear her voice, especially after the exhausting trip to Charlotte. "I didn't wake you, did I?"

"Connor, it's eleven o'clock. That would be ridiculous if you did." She paused. "I've been up for a good ten minutes."

He laughed. "I'm glad I didn't call you when I first wanted to, then."

"When was that?"

"The moment I woke up." It was a confession he was surprised he said out loud, given the amount of time they'd been dating so far. But things with Katie were just different from anything he'd experienced before. "But since you were still working when I called you on the drive home last night, I figured I better wait. Did you finish?"

"I did." He could hear the smile in her voice. "I got the footage from the hay ride— which was the last of it — sent to the Glaciers, and I got the video for tonight's Allred family party finished at about four a.m."

"Congratulations! You didn't drool on the keyboard, accidentally edit in your snoring as the soundtrack, or leave a trail of Z's in the captions, right?"

"Nope," she said rather proudly. "I had enough caffeine in me up until the end. Of course, I can now hear colors and see sounds, so there's that."

"Then I will make sure to only wear the most melodious shades when I see you today." He reached an intersection and pressed the button for the crosswalk. "I am just heading to my car right now, then I've got to stop back at my hotel to grab a bag with the few clothing items I have until my package from Laura shows up." If he'd known it would take so long to ship during the holiday season and with weather delays, he would've just had her pack him a suitcase to take home with him last night.

"Has it already started snowing?"

The light for the crosswalk turned green, and as he started walking, he looked up at the snow that had been lazily falling from the sky when he'd first gone into that store but was now falling with a bit more enthusiasm. "Yep. It's not too crazy yet, but I want to get up the mountain before the roads get bad."

He was most of the way across the sidewalk when he noticed a family that was walking toward the crosswalk. Two kids— a boy and a girl who were both teenagers— and a mom who was holding hands with a dad. *His* dad. "I've got to go. I'll call you when I get close." He hung up the phone and put it in his pocket just as he reached the other side where his dad had stopped in his tracks, as surprised to see Connor as Connor was to see him.

It had been ten years since Connor had last seen him, and all the pain of his dad not only moving out but deciding that he didn't need them anymore hit him fresh.

"Connor," he said, letting go of the woman's hand and taking a step toward him. "It's good to see you. I heard you were traded to the Glaciers."

Connor hadn't known where his dad was living for years. But he knew that Connor was back in Denver? So many questions filled his mind. More than he could take in, making the moment feel overwhelming enough that he couldn't even manage to say anything.

"I, uh, got remarried about a year ago."

Connor's eyes flicked to the woman and then to who he presumed were her kids. A boy and a girl, just like he had the first time around with Connor and Laura. Somehow, this felt like an even bigger betrayal.

"I've wanted to tell you."

"Tell me what? That you found a family to replace us?"

"No, that's— "

"I'm sorry," Connor said. "I've got somewhere I need to be before the roads get bad." Then he turned away from them and hurried toward his car, not even pausing long enough to see the expression on his dad's face. Whatever it was, it was more than he could handle right now.

Why did he have to get traded to *Denver*, of all places?

He felt the buzz of a text and pulled his phone from his pocket. It was a text from his agent.

I caught the game last night. You played well. Sorry, you weren't able to pull a win out of it. That was rough, buddy. Just let me know when you're ready for me to submit that trade request. It could cause strife between you and the GM, especially since they just worked so hard to get you, but it's also good to give them a heads-up that you want to leave so they can keep an eye out for a beneficial trade. But it'd probably be best if you kept it from your teammates. If you don't end up getting traded until the end of the season, you don't want it causing ripples before then.

Connor didn't respond to the text. He just turned his phone off, shoved it into his pocket, and kept on walking.

KATIE

KATIE STOOD beside her mom in their big kitchen, cutting up apples for the pies while her mom rolled out the pie crusts. Three of her sisters had arrived with their families, so the place was already filled with a lot of action, a lot of noise, a lot of delicious scents, and enough Christmas decorations that everything felt exactly like Christmas Eve.

A couple of her nieces were folding the red napkins that went with the Christmas place settings into origami shapes based on some "YouTube research" they'd done, while all the littler cousins were either playing with a car set just under the big Christmas tree or piling on top of a couple of her brothers-in-law.

"You know," Julianne said, leaning in to point at the

apple Katie was slicing, "if you slice along there first, then— "

"I've got this," Katie said. She could do something as simple as slicing an apple without instruction.

She glanced toward the hall leading to her dad's office, waiting for him to come out. And waiting for Connor to arrive— she really thought he would beat her there.

She heard the front door open and looked over to see Jack and Noelle come into the family room. "We just got to see the puppies!" Noelle said while holding up her phone, and Katie rinsed the juice from the apples off her hands and hurried over to see.

"Holly's grandparents are over for Christmas Eve," Noelle said, "but they let us come play with them for a bit."

Katie leaned in to look at pictures of the little fur babies as Noelle swiped through them, several of her nieces and nephews coming in close to see, too.

"Three of the five of them already have their eyes open," Noelle said. "Oh, see this one? She's the one that's going to be ours when she's ready."

"I'm impressed you two are willing to take on training a new puppy so soon after having a baby," Katie said.

"Yeah," Jack said, "we might be a little crazy. Funny story— we were babysitting Aiden and Holly when

Bailey went into labor. When I called them to let them know, they thought it was Noelle who was in labor."

"Oh, I wish I was," Noelle said, putting a hand on her belly. "I'm ready to pop."

"Happy birthday to Noelle," her six-year-old nephew, Porter called out in the cadence of the poem *The Night Before Christmas.*

Katie, along with everyone else in the room called back, "and to Noelle a good night."

She had just made it back to the kitchen to continue with the apple slicing when her dad came out of his office and headed straight toward her, a big smile on his face. She started grinning even before he got there. "You, my daughter, did an excellent job on those videos!"

As the head of brand management, her dad was one of the people who she knew would be the first to see the videos she submitted. "You like them?"

"When I first told you that you were being assigned the player who was traded, do you remember that I assigned them to you because I didn't want to dump it on someone else last minute? That I didn't think it was professional but that I knew you'd be forgiving of that?"

She nodded.

"That wasn't the actual reason why. I didn't want to tell you at the time because I didn't want you to feel the pressure of it, but we assigned the new player to you because out of all the videographers we hired, you were by far the strongest at bringing out the emotion of an event through your videos."

"I was?"

"The franchise is really excited about getting Connor, and they wanted a video that would really sell him to the hearts of the fans. And you knocked it out of the park, just like we guessed you would."

She smiled widely as she took in a big breath that made her feel like she had grown an inch or two.

"It's not my call what gets aired— Advertising and the GM get the ultimate say on that, but I'm betting they'll love it and see the brilliance behind it. I also spelled it out for them just in case."

"Thank you!" she said and gave him a tight hug. She was so deliriously thrilled that it was making her light-headed. She heard the front door open, and she looked over to see Connor as he rounded the corner into the family room. She practically skipped over to him, wrapped her arms around him, and gave him a kiss.

"Wow, you are beaming."

"My dad just watched the video I sent the Glaciers of you, and he loves it."

"Of course he did. You're very good at what you do."

She grinned at him. Creating something that others appreciated gave her a high unlike nothing else. Her smile faltered just a bit, though, as she took in Connor's face. "Is everything okay?"

He smiled, but it didn't feel quite as genuine as his smiles normally did. "Yes, I'm fine. Everything is good. I'm just a little sore from yesterday's game. I'm sorry for taking so long to get here— I decided to get chains on the tires of my rental car. And with the snow that has already fallen, I-seventy was moving painfully slow."

"Happy birthday to Noelle," her nine-year-old niece, Erika called out, and everyone else, including Katie, joined in to say, "And to Noelle a good night."

"Oh, yeah," Katie said, noticing the confused look on Connor's face. "That's a thing here."

He nodded and grinned. As they were all working on dinner and socializing, Katie watched Connor with her family. Katie liked dating, so she'd had plenty of dates at family things over the years. Usually, they kind of hung back, being a spectator on the sidelines. Or stuck to her like glue. Or found one of her brothers-in-law to chat with. How was this man, who had only been in her life and in her family's life for the past eight days, already fitting in with her family so well? Sure, it felt like much more than eight days, but it was still only eight days.

Since he'd arrived, he'd stood side by side with her, cutting vegetables for roasting, racing some teeny cars with the littler kids, playing a board game with the older kids, and chatting and joking around with all of her sisters, their husbands, and her parents.

She hoped that advertising and the GM of the Glaciers would decide to air the footage a lot. And that everyone would see the man that she saw and fall in love with him, too. Then, there would be no way that the Glaciers would ever trade him to another team, and he'd be around for a good long time. Because she wanted this man to be in her life always.

As they set all the dishes of food on the table and everyone made their way over, she wrapped her arms around his waist and smiled up at him. "You are pretty perfect. Do you know that?"

It was Christmas Eve *and* it was Noelle's birthday. The conversations could've revolved around those two subjects as they ate prime rib and maple bacon Brussels sprouts. But since Connor was there, they revolved around hockey and what Katie was like as a kid— one of her family's favorite subjects whenever she brought someone new to the family table.

"When Katie was born," her oldest sister, Becca, said, "I was nine. Me, Hope, and Julianne are each only a year-and-a-half apart and Noelle is three years younger than Julianne. So she had a lot of sisters who really wanted to smother her with help."

"'Smother' was definitely a good word for it," Katie said, and her parents, especially, laughed.

"She tolerated it well enough until she was, what? A year-and-a-half?" Her mom looked at her dad and he nodded, so she continued. "Then one day, Hope was helping Katie to put on her shoes and Katie said, 'No, I do it.' And from that point on, she had to do everything herself."

"And she does mean *everything*," her dad confirmed.

Was that really so bad? She got to be pretty independent and capable at a very young age.

Julianne pointed at Katie with her fork. "I'm pretty sure her first words were 'No, I do it."

Noelle nodded. "It kind of became her anthem."

Katie grimaced and snuck a peek at Connor. He was chuckling along with everyone else, then said, "It's probably why she's so good at everything she does."

"Thank you!" Katie said, feeling vindicated and giving pointed looks to her siblings. "Also, thank you for telling that story instead of the story where I got into the penguin habitat at the zoo that you told the last time I brought a date to Thanksgiving."

"Oh, that was a good one," Corbin said.

"No," Ben said, "it was the chaos caused by getting her back out that made the story great."

As everyone laughed, reliving probably both their enjoyment at hearing the story and at seeing her date's expressions as they all told the story in detail, Connor leaned in close to her ear, tickling it and sending a happy shiver straight to her heart as he said. "I'm going to want to hear that story later."

"And deprive my family the joy of telling it to you at some future family dinner?"

He chuckled. "Fair enough." But something still seemed off, and she didn't know what it was.

After dinner was finished and cleaned up, all twelve adults, ten kids, and her parents' dog, Captain, made their way to the couches or the fluffy rug in front of it so they could watch Katie's annual Christmas video. It was her favorite part of their celebrations because it brought everything together. All their activities, gatherings, and everyone's thoughts. She could see how much it made their family bonds stronger and helped everyone to realize how grateful they were for each other.

She woke her laptop that sat on a shelf by the TV, turned on the TV, and went into her laptop's settings to connect to it. It gave an error that it couldn't connect using WiFi, and her brother-in-law Cory started to get off the couch, saying "I can help."

"I've got this," Katie said, a little annoyed.

"No, I do it!" Becca said, and everyone laughed.

Katie had just forgotten that she had put her laptop into airplane mode to minimize distractions while she'd been editing, and it only took an extra two seconds to turn the WiFi back on, and then everything worked.

In Katie's defense, she kind of had a right to get bugged by everyone always wanting to help. They always assumed that since they were older, they knew more.

And since she was the youngest, she needed extra help with everything, like she was incompetent. *She wasn't.*

She brought up the video, made it full screen, pressed play, then hurried to her spot on the couch closest to the laptop, and snuggled in right next to Connor.

Since Jack and Noelle were about to become parents, she started by showing an interview she'd shot with the two of them a few weeks ago when they had decorated the gingerbread cars for the train at the side of the room.

"We are so excited because this is the first Christmas that we'll be spending in our new house!" Noelle said. "We probably won't be able to say that it's our first Christmas with a new baby, but you never know when this little one is going to come."

"But whenever he does," Jack said, "we are ready. The house is all ready. His nursery is ready. We are... well, we're not exactly ready, but we're excited and as prepared as we can be."

Noelle gave him the sweetest smile, then said, "And the timing couldn't be more perfect if we had planned it. We fell in love this time of year, we got married this time of year..."

"Noelle's birthday is this time of year..."

"Happy birthday to Noelle," her dad said loudly, and everyone, including Connor, replied back with "and to Noelle a good night!"

It was bound to happen at that point in the video, so

Katie had included a few seconds of Jack and Noelle just smiling at each other, not saying anything, so her family wouldn't miss words while they said it.

And then, with almost perfect timing, if she did say so herself, Noelle said, "And now our baby is going to have a birthday at this time of year, too."

The next several clips were of her nieces and nephews and her sisters and their husbands. She liked sitting in the spot at the edge of everyone so she could see all their faces as they watched the video. It was how she determined whether she hit the mark on what she chose to include, and seeing them enjoy it was the best kind of payment for all her work.

The clip came up that she'd gotten of Aiden sitting next to Connor on the hay ride, with him saying. "My uncle Jack fell in love on this hay ride two Christmases ago," and she felt Connor chuckle at the memory. Then it cut to Jack and Noelle all snuggled up together, Jack kissing Noelle's temple. Then she had the part where Aiden said, "And my mom fell in love" with Holly interrupting to say "with my dad" before Aiden finished "last Christmas," and showed Rachel and Nick sneaking a kiss as they walked from the hay ride toward a house they'd be caroling at.

She had debated including the part where Holly said, "Maybe you can fall in love this year," followed by a clip of her and Connor together. But they hadn't actually said the L-word to each other yet. She wasn't sure why because she definitely felt it. Maybe it was because eight days— even if it felt like it was fifty— just seemed too soon.

Plus, if she had included every clip of Connor in this video that she wanted to, a good fifty percent of the video would be just him. To keep herself from doing just that, she put all those clips in a separate video to enjoy later.

Instead, she went to a clip of her parents saying how much they enjoyed seeing their family grow and find love and happiness and watching everyone figure out what they were really good at.

She also included a clip she got of Holly saying that Bailey had five of the cutest puppies, then showed those puppies. She figured that since Jack and Noelle were getting one of those puppies and that Rachel and her family were keeping at least one, those puppies were going to be in family Christmas videos for years to come.

Her stomach started getting fluttery as one of her favorite parts came up— all four of her sisters standing side by side, near the end of the Santa Hat activity. Hope said, "The most surprising thing about this year's Santa hat activity was that Katie drew dinner *and it was really good!*"

She grinned at Connor and he grinned right back and then gave her a quick peck on the lips as everyone in the room laughed. She was already enjoying that trophy sitting on a shelf in her living room, and she was going to proudly display it all year.

She also included an interview she'd gotten with Connor. It was right after Erika and Sadie had presented him with the tree their family had decorated so he could have it in his hotel room. Connor had a very wide, very genuine smile on his face, and he was clearly thrilled about the tree he was holding.

"This might be the coolest thing anyone has ever done for me. Thank you for making such an awesome tree and for giving it to me." Katie glanced at Becca and her family and could see that they were all beaming, just like they had that night. "And I would like to thank Reid and Elizabeth and every single member of the Allred family for inviting me into your home and into your family's traditions before you even knew me. It means a lot to have a family to celebrate with when I can't be with my own."

A chorus of *Awws* sounded in the room. Connor put his arm around Katie and pulled her close, kissing the side of her head. Every time Katie watched this part while she was editing and as she was watching it now, she felt the same emotions she had felt when Connor had gotten down to Erika's and Sadie's heights and thanked them— like she was being swept off her feet.

She had only known Connor for a few hours at that

point, and she was already more gone for him than anyone she'd ever dated. Did she know that night how hopelessly in love she was about to fall?

She always included in the video an interview with herself, and in this clip, she had taken on the hay ride, she'd handed the camera to Noelle, who aimed it back at Katie. "One of my favorite things this year has been how Connor sang so enthusiastically while we were caroling that it inspired Captain to do the same."

And then she showed a clip of Captain caroling, seeming to pour his soul into it. At hearing it, Captain sat up from where he was nestled among the kids on the floor and sang right along with himself. Everyone's laughter made her smile. That was what she went for in these videos— a trade-off between the laughter and the *Awws*.

"That," she said in her interview, "and being with everyone as we watched the skits at the Santa Hat activity." She cut to a clip of Julianne and her family pretending to be on a Christmas cooking show, just as Ben "stirred" his dough using a battery-powered drill, their four-year-old's eyes going wide as he stirred his with a socket wrench. Everyone laughed now and in the video clip, and in both places, she could easily pick out Connor's laugh the most. She loved that laugh.

She ended with her parents saying how much they loved spending Christmas with everyone and got a hearty applause. *This* was why she made videos. Not because she got praise, but because it led everyone to feel all the emotions that compelled them to clap enthusiastically. They weren't clapping for her; they were clapping for the experience that they enjoyed. And that was everything she hoped for.

All the little kids had bedtimes soon, so her dad slipped out to grab the sleigh bells he kept in the garage and ring them in front of the house, causing all the little kids to jump up and scramble to gather everything they had brought, put on their coats and shoes, so they could hurry home and get in bed before Santa arrived at their house.

Connor pulled Katie close, his arms wrapped around her, and she snuggled into him. She was still feeling the high of her dad watching the videos she'd submitted to the Glaciers of Connor and of her family watching the Christmas video. But the last few days had been insanely busy, and she was exhausted. It was wonderful to just relax and melt into him, feeling the strength of his arms. He kissed along her jaw, and when he got close to her ear, he breathed, "You truly are incredible at what you do."

His words sent goosebumps all over her body. "Thank you," she said and pressed her lips against his.

sixteen

CONNOR

AS EVERYONE WAS GETTING ready to leave, Katie's dad looked out the living room windows, and everyone else crowded around to look, too. A good amount of snow had fallen. A foot, maybe?

"It looks like the snow plows are keeping up just fine." He turned to look at everyone. "But they're expecting it to keep dumping for quite a while. Will you all text the group chat when you get home and let us know you made it safely?"

Katie's sisters said yes and they, along with Katie's brothers-in-law and her nieces and nephews, all said their goodbyes. He was sure he heard at least twice as many callouts of "Merry Christmas!" as there were people present.

And then they all shuffled out into the snow, leaving

just Katie, her parents, and Connor in the home. Without everyone's shoes and coats strewn about, Katie noticed his bag. "Oh! I didn't even think to show you to your room when you first got here!"

He picked up his bag and followed her down the hallway and into a bedroom. He had kind of expected a typical guest bedroom— white or cream-colored walls, a queen bed with a comforter in a neutral color and pattern, a dresser, maybe a generic piece of art hanging on a wall, but not much else. Instead, this was a bedroom filled with personality and items.

The walls were painted lavender. The bed was queen-sized, but the comforter was teal and purple and had a handful of fuzzy throw pillows. A dozen square, black-and-white framed photos hung on the wall above the bed. Inspirational quotes about dreams and creativity were on the walls and on objects on the dresser and shelves. A few trophies stood tall on shelves.

"Was this your room?"

"Yeah," Katie said, scratching the back of her head. "My parents kept it the same because I stayed here on weekends and summers when I came home from college. I don't know why they didn't change it into a legit guest room when I got my own place like they said they were going to." Then she laughed. "Maybe because I haven't come to pack all this old stuff up yet. I kind of forgot they asked me to." Her eyes went wide as she flipped a frame on the dresser to face down. "I probably should have."

He dropped his bag on the floor and wandered around to check everything out. The place might not have been Katie's for a while, but it still felt like the spirit of her was here. Like he was getting a glimpse into the younger version of her.

The pictures above the bed were a mix of beautiful landscapes, candid shots of family and friends, and close-ups of nature's intricate details. All proof that she'd been good with a camera for a while. More photos, some sentimental notes from friends, a teacher's scrawled encouragement torn from the corner of some kind of assignment, and a few fortunes pulled from cookies lay under the glass on top of the wood on the bedside table.

He walked over to the shelves and saw a few things he hadn't noticed when he first walked in— a snow globe, probably from a family vacation, a ceramic hand-print she'd made as a child, framed photos of her with her sisters, and a few photography and videography books. And right next to that, something that he was pretty sure was a photo album. He put one finger at the top of the spine. "Can I look at this?"

"Um, sure. I don't really remember what's in it, but I guess we'll find out."

The two of them sat on the edge of her bed and he opened it up. In the first picture, she was maybe ten and had a butterfly on her finger that she was holding out to the camera. A quick glance at the other photos on the page told him that this was a mix of random pictures from throughout her childhood.

He asked plenty of questions, and she told him story after story. It was mesmerizing to hear about her childhood. Seeing how she looked at the world. Hearing about what was important to her. He didn't even realize that it was getting late until she tried to hold back a yawn in the middle of a sentence. He grabbed his phone. "It's nearly midnight!" He couldn't believe how fast time flew whenever he was with Katie. Why couldn't it slow down instead?

Katie nodded. "And I'm betting Santa passed right by us." She stood up and studied him, her hands on her hips. "When I was a teenager, I felt like a queen being able to have a bed this big— it was one of the perks of being the youngest— but I'm betting you won't feel the same. You're used to what? A Texas king-sized bed?"

Connor laughed, then flopped himself onto the bed, linking his hands behind his head. "This one is going to do just fine."

"Your feet are hanging off the end."

"That's perfect because my feet get hot when I sleep. Plus, I'll get to lay here and wonder what you were like as a teen. If I have any trouble sleeping, I can look at the pictures on your walls, the things on your shelves, and maybe come to a few conclusions."

Katie ran her hands over her face. "I really should've come and packed stuff up before now."

Looking through the photo album had taken his mind off everything. Talking about her as a high-schooler, though, got him back to thinking of when he was, too, and the school Christmas dance where he ruined her dress and caused countless other problems.

One of the many reasons why he arrived later yesterday than he had planned was because after seeing his dad, he decided he needed to spend some time with the standing punching bag in the hotel's gym. But even that didn't help keep his mind from going right back to his teenage years when he realized that his dad found his new life so much more interesting than a life with his family.

The shower after and the painstakingly slow drive up the mountain didn't take his mind away from it, either. So once he'd gotten to Mountain Springs, he'd taken a detour and driven past the house his family had lived in back then. He didn't know why— he wasn't expecting it to give him closure or anything. And all it did was re-open old wounds.

"Are you sure you're okay?" Katie was studying him intently.

He nodded. "It was just hard being back in Charlotte,

seeing my old teammates, talking with my best friend on the team. Things like that."

She placed a hand gently on his shoulder. "Do you want to talk about it?"

He shook his head.

But at the same time, between Vaughan bringing up the rumor that the Explorers were looking for a new right wing and his agent asking when he wanted to submit the trade request, all of the trade stuff was working its way through his head, too.

Did he want to have his agent put in the trade request? Eight days ago, if he had known his dad was in Denver or if he had run into him then, the answer would've been a resounding yes. He couldn't keep having those old wounds opened. He had told himself that he could make it here because he thought his dad had moved on far from this place. Like to another country, as Laura had last heard. But now, he knew that he could possibly run into him anywhere. His dad always liked hockey— he could even be at his games.

He was surprised it affected him so much. After that incident in his junior year, his mom got him into a great therapist. He thought he'd worked through everything. But apparently, working through issues didn't mean they couldn't resurface when unexpectedly facing them again. And he felt like every time he saw his dad, he would be sent right back to that place where he was angry all the time. When he hated who he was as a person.

Yes, his dad was in Denver. But Katie was, too.

And he could really use her level head and logical thinking to help him work through everything.

"Actually, I would." He stood, and she took a seat on the edge of the bed. "When we moved away from Denver, I never wanted to come back. In the NHL, you can't have a No Trade clause in your contract until you are twenty-seven or have played seven seasons. I had planned to have my agent negotiate a *No Trade to Denver* clause in my contract the moment I could. But then I got traded just a few weeks before I could have.

"So, I told my agent the day I got here that I was interested in putting in a trade request. It's not the same thing, and it doesn't guarantee anything— it just lets the franchise know that I'm not happy here and want to leave. They don't tend to love having a player who doesn't want to be on their team, so they'll usually look to trade them.

"He hasn't put in the request yet, though, because it can cause friction, but he texted me earlier today to ask when I want to." He paced over a little rectangle of her floor, looking down at the carpet as he tried to put it all into words.

"And I do like the Glaciers. It's a great team. Good teammates, a coach who knows how to push us, supportive management, and an incredible fan base. I'm just not sure if I can play my best here. There are too many things I keep running into that take me back to that person I hated being."

He let out a long breath, stopped pacing, and looked up at Katie. "But I don't know— what do you think?"

He had been so focused on trying to put all that was swirling around in his head into words that he hadn't even noticed what his words were doing to her. And right now, she had an incredible amount of pain on her face. Slowly and carefully, she said, "I think that if you're so unhappy here, you should put in the trade request."

Taking two steps toward her, he knelt down just in front of her knees. "Katie, listen. You know this isn't about you at all, right?"

"Yeah, I get that it's not about me. I didn't before this conversation, but I do now." She stood. "Listen, it's late, and it's probably still snowing, so I should really go."

He hadn't even been thinking about the snow. He pulled out his phone to check the weather and road conditions as he followed her out of the room. All of the lights in the house were off except for the one nearest the front door, so her parents must've already gone to bed. Which wasn't surprising, given the time.

"The snow plows are no longer keeping up," he said as they reached the living room, still scanning info on his phone. "It says that emergency vehicles can't get to people who are stuck, and they recommend not driving."

She was still putting on her coat, though. The feelings of comfort and bliss that had surrounded them as they'd looked through the photo album were gone, replaced by an uneasy tenseness.

"You should stay," he said. "You can sleep in your old bed— I can sleep on that giant sectional couch in the family room."

She finished zipping up her coat and turned to him. "Connor, my parents offered you a place to stay. Not only if there was any 'room at the inn.' You have a reserved room. I do not."

He stepped closer to her. "I really don't mind."

Instead of closing the gap between them even more, as he had hoped, she turned and grabbed one of her boots and put it on. "Connor, I'm not staying."

He wanted her to stay because he wanted to know that things between them were okay. But even more than that, he wanted her to be okay. And going out into the snowstorm wasn't the best way to do that. He walked over to the window and moved the curtains to look out. While they'd been talking and Katie had been telling him stories about her childhood, the amount of snow on the ground had doubled. It always amazed him how the skies could dump so much snow and do it without making a sound.

He turned to face her. "Would you like me to drive you home?" He grinned, trying to lighten the mood enough that she would take him up on his offer. "I have chains on my tires now."

"I don't need my hand held. I've been driving on snow-covered roads since I was sixteen. I am not inexperienced."

They sometimes got snow in Charlotte, but it was rare and never more than just an inch or two, so she definitely had him beat in experience. He'd spent a couple of winters living in Mountain Springs, though, so he knew how bad the roads could get. He motioned toward the window. "But that's a lot of snow. There's probably close to a foot of fresh stuff on the roads. How about you at least take my car?"

She just gave him a look before tugging on one of her gloves.

He held up his hands. "I know, I know. You've got this."

"I do," she said firmly and got out her keys.

He knew enough about Katie to know that trying to convince her even further would only backfire. "Will you at least text me when you get home to let me know you made it safely?"

She nodded and said, "I will," which at least lightened the heaviness of his heart just a bit. She turned to leave but then turned back. "And Connor?"

"Yeah?"

"Merry Christmas," she said, then took a couple of steps toward him and gave him a kiss on the cheek before turning and walking out of the house. He couldn't help but feel like his heart was leaving with her.

seventeen

KATIE

KATIE'S HEAD was a jumbled mess as she walked out of her parents' house, leaving Connor behind. She got a text from her dad a couple of hours ago saying that they were going to bed, but if much more snow fell and she wanted help shoveling the driveway so she could get her car out, to just call or knock on their bedroom door. Or to feel free to not deal with the snow at all and just stay the night.

She didn't knock or call. But when she got outside, she saw that her dad had already shoveled around her car and all the driveway behind it. Several more inches had fallen since he had. She got into her car to find a plate of food with a note from her mom taped to it.

Leftovers! Your car is at least as cold as the fridge, so I figured I'd bring them out so you didn't forget them.

Maybe she should start wearing a pin to family things that said *Just because I'm the youngest doesn't mean I'm still a kid.* She squeezed her eyes shut for a moment as a little voice in her head said, "Your parents would do those things for any of their kids." She ran her hands over her face, then pulled out of the driveway and started heading toward home. She was just upset because of what happened with Connor.

Why did she have to fall so fully for a guy who had one foot back in Charlotte and the other foot looking for a place away from Denver to land? It had only been eight days since he'd run into her at that department store, yet she already knew him so much better than she'd known any one of her past boyfriends. She already loved him more than any past boyfriend. How much more would she have a month from now, a year from now, if given the chance?

With every previous guy that she dated, there was always a moment when she thought, "Do I want to continue dating him? Or am I ready to move on?" Connor was the only guy who had ever stepped into her life that she'd had thoughts of spending her life with.

She had recently edited the part of his videos when they'd been heading to the community center to judge the gingerbread houses, and the five-year-old boy stopped to ask him questions about hockey. It was one of her favorite clips, and as she re-watched it several times, she realized that somewhere along the way, she had started imagining a life with Connor.

Maybe they'd get married and live near the arena for the first while so he didn't have far to commute, and she would expand her videography business to Denver. On home game days, he'd go to practice in the mornings while she edited videos, and then, he'd come home in the afternoon for a nap to power up for the game. On days when she didn't have too many deadlines, she would crawl into bed and snuggle up in the covers with him. And then she would go to his games in the evenings, taking Emmalee with her, and she'd cheer for him until she lost her voice.

And then, after a couple of years, they'd decide that it was time to start a family, and she'd get pregnant. And maybe they'd decide that they wanted to raise their child in a smaller town, and they'd head back to Mountain Springs, and maybe add a couple more kids to the mix. Because he was so great with kids, he would be an amazing dad. They would buy them little hockey uniforms and teach them how to skate so they could experience the sport that their dad loved so much.

It was a life she really thought she'd love. It wasn't a dream she'd had for long, but it was so vivid and felt so right. And so new. She'd never been able to picture herself having a life with anyone before. Maybe because she'd never met anyone who was so giving and fun and up for anything. Or so thoughtful and helpful and a good cook. Or have a face that she could never tire of staring at.

Her tires slipped a little as she slowed for a stop sign, so she pumped the brakes several times to slow down but didn't come to a complete stop out of fear of not being able to go again. They slipped at the next turn, too. She might have had a ton of experience driving in snow, but she wasn't actually sure she'd driven in this deep of snow before. It was slowing her enough that she probably hadn't gotten over 10 miles per hour since she left.

She turned onto a road where the snow was a little deeper, and she worried that her little car wasn't going to make it. But she just took it slow and was able to keep moving. She was squinting to try to tell where the edge of the road was since everything was covered in white, then saw a little something that wasn't white. In fact, it was moving. She squinted a little more, trying to see it through the snow.

It was a dog! He was crouched under a small bush in an area with empty lots and no houses around. The bush had gotten completely covered in snow, leaving only a small window between the snow on the ground and the snow on the bush for him to peek out of. She pulled her car to what she thought was probably the side of the road and put it into park but left the engine running. Then she trudged through the snow to the snow-covered shrub.

The poor little pup was trembling. Maybe from the cold, maybe from being alone in a storm like this. Maybe both. She pushed the snow out of the way and reached in to grab the small dog. "*Shh. Shh*," she said as she wrapped it in her arms and carried it to her car. "Everything's going to be okay. Oh, you must be so cold."

Once back in her car, she blasted the heater, grabbed some of the napkins she kept stashed in her glove box, and dried off the little guy's fur as best as she could. The longer he was on her lap, getting warmer, the more he stopped trembling. She put him on the passenger's side floor, then pulled up the plastic wrap from the corner of the plate her mom had made for her, took out a piece of the meat, put the rest of the plate in her back seat, and started tearing the meat into chunks.

The dog devoured it. "Wow, you must've been so hungry. Let's get you someplace warm, and I'll get you some more food."

She put her seatbelt on, put her car into drive, and gave it a bit of gas. The tires just spun. *Don't panic.* She gave it the tiniest bit of gas, took her foot off the pedal, and then gave it the tiniest bit more. She kept repeating the process, getting the car to gently rock, giving it slightly more gas each time. For a moment, she thought it was going to work. Until the wheels spun again and made her slide a bit.

"It looks like I'm going to have to dig us out. You stay in here and keep warm, okay?"

She popped the trunk of her car and rifled around for anything she could use as a shovel. There wasn't, but if she wanted to go hammocking or roast some marshmallows, she was set. She did have a blanket, so she got back into the car, made a little nest with it on the passenger's seat, and put the dog in it. Then she opened the back door, flipped the plate of food upside down onto the plastic wrap, then removed the plate, and wrapped the plastic around the food. A paper plate wasn't the best shovel ever, but it was better than nothing.

Using the plate was only a little bit helpful. But really, using her foot worked better. She cleared a path around the tires as best as she could, then got in and tried again. It moved an inch or two, then seemed just as stuck.

She just needed to warm up and then she could try again. She pulled the dog onto her lap, and he snuggled right into her, so she grabbed the blanket and wrapped it around them both. Her phone binged with a text, so she picked it up from its spot in front of the gear shift.

Connor: You never texted to let me know you made it home safe. Is everything okay?

She couldn't say that she got stuck. Not after he warned her about the conditions of the roads and practically begged her not to go. She would get herself free and make it home soon. She looked down at the dog in her lap and the blanket wrapped around them both.

Katie: Sorry! I'm snuggled up all nice and warm.

Connor: So good to hear. Sleep well.

The moment she was warm, she got out and tried to clear away more snow from the front of the car. But it was just falling so fast that it was undoing her work. She cleared the snow from around the exhaust, too. She knew better than to let it get high enough back there to cause problems.

Still, the car wouldn't move at all.

After blasting the heater for several minutes to warm back up, she got out and cleared away more snow with her feet and her gloved hands. This time when she tried to drive away, the tires just spun from the start until they started to slide, taking her car off the shoulder of the road, and getting it more stuck. She hit the steering wheel with her palms and let out a shout of frustration that scared the dog. "Oh, I'm so sorry." She gathered it into her arms. "It's going to be okay. I promise."

She turned the car off to preserve the gas she had. She would just turn it back on whenever she got too cold. She wrapped the blanket around her again and tucked the dog into her lap. Then she picked up her phone and texted Emmalee.

> Katie: Are you awake?

About two seconds later, her phone rang, showing Emmalee's face. "I am, actually. Can't sleep. I think it's leftover from days of trying to wait up for Santa, I guess. Probably because I'm back home in my old room. Why are you awake?"

"My car got stuck in the snow on my way back to our apartment."

"Oh my gosh! Have you called for help?"

"No. Emergency services already said they can't help motorists because the conditions are too bad. You know how it is when there's a big storm here. They'll slowly get dug out and will eventually get around to everyone who needs help. I just need to wait out the storm."

"You can't just wait it out in your car overnight!"

"Sure I can. I had a spare blanket in my trunk. My parents sent me home with leftovers, so it's not like I'm going to starve." Even though Emmalee couldn't see her, she motioned to the food in the back seat and noticed that the dog must've gone back for more while she was outside clearing away snow. The plastic was open and the food was spread all over it and her back seat, and the rest of the meat was gone. She gave the dog a scolding look, but she couldn't really be mad at the cute thing. "And I still have a fourth a tank of gas, so I can turn my car on for heat now and then."

"Until the snow gets higher than your exhaust pipe and you accidentally carbon monoxide yourself to death."

"Not going to happen, because I just keep going back there to clear it away. Plus, I have a little dog to keep me company. We're keeping each other warm."

"What dog?"

"*The* cutest little honey-colored cairn terrier. He was trapped in the snow and freezing, so I helped him."

"You got stuck in the snow because you were trying to save a dog?"

"Listen, Emmalee. He was so scared and cold that he was trembling!"

"Our apartment doesn't even allow pets!"

"Oh, he already has an owner. He's got a collar with one of those tags where there's a chip and they can scan it to see who the owner is. So I can't call them to say I have their dog. But Emmalee, he was lost in the snow! He probably belongs to a family with kids. Come morning, they're going to get a call saying that their dog was found and it's going to be the best Christmas present ever.

"If I didn't save him, then they were going to wake up Christmas morning to find out that their dog died. *On Christmas Day.* They'd be scarred for life. I had to save him. I don't know what his name is, but I decided to call him Biscuit."

Emmalee was quiet for a moment, then said, "I probably would've done the same." She paused a moment, then added, "When I said 'the same,' I meant rescuing him. I would've named him Zamboni."

"Of course you would have."

"Okay, then, we need to get both you and Biscuit rescued. Call your parents! They might know someone with a snowmobile or even a Sno-cat."

"It's the middle of the night— I'm not going to call them. Especially because I made such a stink about not wanting help."

"Katie."

"And if I did, they'd have to call around for help. Again: middle of the night. And not just that, but the middle of the night on Christmas Eve."

"Then call Connor."

"When I left, things weren't exactly going well between us. He told me that he had already asked his agent about putting in a trade request and his agent was just waiting on him to say when." She rubbed Biscuit's fur by his ears, and the dog laid his head in her lap, closing his eyes.

Emmalee gasped. "He did not."

"He did. Here I am, completely falling for him and thinking that he feels the same about me. But if he was considering *asking* to leave, then he wasn't. I don't think he cares about us nearly as much as I thought he did."

"How is that even possible? The man made brides-maid bouquets for you! Are you so heartbroken right now?"

"I am. I really thought he was the one."

"I can't believe he would just send you out into a storm, though, and not even care."

"Oh, he cared." She was getting really cold again, so she turned the car on to let the heater run for a bit and ran the windshield wipers a couple of times so she could see.

There was a slight pause before Emmalee said, "He offered to drive you home or follow you to make sure you made it, but you told him no."

"Something like that." It was stupid. She had just been bugged by everyone offering to help with things she could do herself. And then when she found out that Connor wanted to leave, it was just too much, and her agitation made her react in a way that she'd known had been stupid at the time. Still, though, she did it.

"Did he at least ask you to text him when you made it home?"

"Yep. And when I didn't and he texted to ask if I made it, I told him I was snuggled up all nice and warm."

"You *lied* to him?!"

"It wasn't a lie! I was snuggled up all nice and warm with Biscuit."

"Did you purposely make him believe something that wasn't true?"

"Okay, fine, I lied and it was a really stupid choice. Listen, Emmalee. I didn't call to worry you or make you feel like you needed to solve this. I just called to see if you would commiserate with me. So... commiserate with me?"

There was a long pause. "Emmalee?"

Still nothing, so Katie looked at her phone. The screen was black. She tapped on it a few times, but it still didn't light up. She pressed the power button, but nothing. She held it down, and the *No battery* symbol lit up. "No!" How could it have died without her noticing that it was getting low on power? Then she remembered that freezing temperatures drained a phone battery faster.

It was okay. She would just keep getting out every thirty minutes or so to make sure the area behind the exhaust was clear of snow. Then she'd try to wait fifteen minutes between each time she turned the car on to blast the furnace so the gas would last as long as possible. It would be a very long night, but she could get help in the morning.

It turned out that she couldn't wait fifteen minutes between each time she turned on the car, though. Her boots, socks, the bottom half of her pants, her gloves, and the bottom half of her coat sleeves were so wet from trying to clear the snow, and it made her so cold. Her hood was pretty wet, too.

Why had she not just called Connor while she had the chance?

She shivered as she pulled the blanket tighter, and then she petted Biscuit again. "We're going to make it through this, little guy. We'll be okay." She just needed to keep saying it, and it would be true.

CONNOR

CONNOR COULDN'T BELIEVE how dense he'd been to ask Katie her opinion on him putting in a trade request. He should've expected that she would look at it through the lens of the two of them. When he'd said that it wasn't about her, he'd meant that his wanting to go had nothing to do with her. Now that he was looking at it from her perspective, he understood that she took it to mean that she didn't make a difference in his wanting to stay.

He wished he could rewind the night and try again. Actually, that he could rewind the previous day and a half. Between going to Charlotte, playing such a rough game against his old team, and seeing his dad again in the same city where he was living, he had been just throwing so many things in the "Why I should leave" column in his head.

Of course, he put Katie on the "Why I should stay" side. But his focus had been on the longer side— the one with the fresh emotions he'd been experiencing in quick succession. What he should've been asking himself was "Could I handle being traded away from Katie?" The answer to that was an unequivocal *No*. He had no interest in being away from her. If he hadn't lost perspective so much and just asked himself that question from the start, he wouldn't have dwelt on everything else. It all would've fallen away as insignificant.

He stayed up and worried about Katie until he got the text from her saying that she made it home. But as much as he tried, he still couldn't fall asleep. At one point, he considered calling Vaughan, or even Erik, just so he could talk through everything. But he wasn't about to call them in the middle of the night. Especially on Christmas Eve, and especially because they both had wives whom he would also be waking up with his call.

Eventually, he must've fallen asleep because he woke from dreaming about ice melting under his skates to the sound of a phone call. He reached for the phone, disoriented and clumsy. But he managed to pry his eyes open to see that the screen showed a time of 3:11 a.m. and a phone call from the name *Emmalee*. It took a moment for his brain to wake up and realize it was Katie's friend.

When he'd stopped at the flower shop to get Katie's address, they had swapped phone numbers in case he couldn't find their apartment.

As soon as he answered the phone, Emmalee said, "Katie is stuck in the snow."

He sat up straight. "What? Isn't she home?"

"Nope! She's stubborn and stuck on the side of the road with a dog."

'With a dog?" He put the phone on speaker so he could start changing.

"Apparently a really cute one that she rescued and is calling Biscuit. We have our locations shared with each other, so when she first told me she was stuck, I went in to see where she was and took a screenshot. I'm texting it to you now. Before our conversation was over, the line went dead. I don't know if there's a problem with cell reception because of the storm, or if her battery died, or what. And I'm at my parents in Lakewood and I-seventy is closed, so I can't get there to help."

He'd changed into pants, put on socks, and checked to make sure that he got the screenshot. Then he said, "No, stay where you are. I'm going to go to her. I'll keep you updated."

After taking two steps toward his door, he went back and grabbed the pajama pants he'd just taken off and an extra pair of socks. Then he rushed to the home's front door and put on the boots he bought just a day ago in anticipation of this storm, tucking his pants into them. Then he put on his coat, gloves, and hat, grabbed his keys, and went outside.

A snow shovel was leaning against the garage door, so he grabbed it, tossed it into his back seat, and started driving toward where the map said Katie was.

The roads were so much worse now than when Katie had left. Even with chains on his tires, he worried he wouldn't make it through some parts. It was just so deep. The going was slow, but he made sure not to come to a complete stop anywhere.

The road he was coming up to hadn't been plowed as recently as the one he was on, and he worried about the extra depth. He glanced at the map to see if there was any alternate road he could take to get him from where he was to the dot where Katie was, but he couldn't see any other options. So he turned onto it.

His car felt so much more bogged down. He kept his speed steady, making sure he wasn't pushing on the gas too much. His tires were still turning, likely only because of the chains.

And then suddenly they weren't.

He tried giving the car a little bit of gas and then tried to get it rocking back and forth to compress the snow around the tires enough to get some traction, but it was no use. The snow was just too deep. After putting the car into park, he pulled off a glove, grabbed his phone, and looked at the screenshot. Katie had to be only about a block and a half away from him. He could walk to her, but simply getting to her wasn't enough. She needed to be someplace warm, and there was no way to drive.

There weren't any houses nearby, and this area didn't seem familiar to him at all. It could be because everything was covered in snow so nothing looked normal. He switched out of the screenshot and went into a GPS map on his phone where he could look at a bigger area or zoom in.

He looked between the map and his surroundings. Currently, he was about a block away from a cross street, and Katie was not far from the corner going right. Going left at that corner and about a block down, though, was the rink he used to practice at as a teen when he lived in Mountain Springs. He swiped over to his phone's contacts— maybe he still had the owner's contact information. The man used to let him practice in the early mornings before they opened and just hid a key outside for him.

He did! He tapped to call him. After several rings, a man's groggy voice came on the line. "Hello?"

"Knox? This is Connor Greene. I don't know if you still remember me from when I used to skate— "

"Connor! Of course, I still remember you." His voice was sounding much more alive, the grogginess slowly falling from it. "Remember how I had all the jerseys from the current Glaciers' team up on the wall in the rink?"

"I do."

"When the Thunderstorm signed you, I was one of the first people to buy your jersey. It's been hanging next to them ever since. I tell everyone who comes in that you used to skate here."

"Really?" The man remembered him? And not in a bad way?

"Yep. And you better believe that I have a Glaciers one with your name on the back on pre-order already."

"I am really touched. Thank you." He glanced out at the white landscape and the snow that was still falling at the same relentless pace. "The reason I'm calling you is that I'm stuck in the snow."

"Oh no. Do you need me to come rescue you?"

"No. The roads are too bad to help. I was actually driving to rescue someone else when I got stuck. A woman that I've realized I'm in love with, right after foolishly causing some damage to our relationship that I'm hoping isn't irreparable. She's not far from where I am, which is close to the rink. I'm wondering if you still keep a key outside."

"Oh, for sure. It's in the same place, actually."

"In the broken grout between the bricks right below the window near the back?"

"That's it. When you get her there, take her to my office. It should be unlocked. It's the warmest place in the building, and there's a space heater."

"Thank you so much. I really appreciate it."

"You're welcome. Oh, and Connor? I'm still rooting for you."

Connor could tell that the man was referring to more than just hockey, and his voice came out a little choked as he said, "Thank you."

He stuffed the pajama pants and socks into the front of his coat, put his glove back on, grabbed the shovel from his back seat, and started shoveling his way toward Katie. The snow was deep, and not only was trudging through it going to be difficult, but he needed to keep from getting so wet that he wouldn't be as helpful to Katie.

He wanted to run to Katie, yet he was making his way toward her so slowly. To distract himself from the anxiety of needing to get to her quickly— she had been out there for hours already— he named something he loved about her with each shovelful of snow. *She's competitive.* Shovel. *She's creative.* Shovel. *She believes family is important.* Shovel.

Shovelful after shovelful, he thought about her. *She is a good friend. She's talented. She's skilled. She helps out others. She makes me laugh. She helps me to see the good in everything. She keeps me grounded. She's tenacious. She has strong convictions. She's thoughtful. She's strong-willed and persistent. I like the way her mind works. She makes me feel like I can be myself.*

Why did he ever think that leaving this place was something he could possibly do? It wasn't. If he'd gotten his head away from the negative things that had bombarded him in such quick succession, none of this would've happened.

Finally, he neared her car. It had slid off the road and was sitting on an angle, so it would likely take a tow truck to pull it out. And there was so much snow on top of it that she must feel like she was inside an ice box.

He went up to her door and wiped away the snow from her window. She sat in the driver's seat, wrapped in a blanket, hunched over and shivering. She didn't seem to notice him at first, so he knocked on the glass with the knuckle of his gloved right finger. Her head immediately spun toward the sound, and he watched as recognition and then relief washed over her face, followed by a smile. It was an exhausted smile, but that smile lifted his spirits like nothing else.

She was okay. Not great, obviously, but she couldn't have managed a smile unless she was at least okay.

He shoveled the area in front of her door, then opened it, and she said, "Connor, you came!"

Oh. She looked *very* cold. He gave her a smile he hoped was encouraging and didn't show the worry he felt. "My car got stuck, too, but I know somewhere warm we can go to wait for help. It's just over a block away, maybe a block and a half. Do you think you can walk?"

She nodded, then unwrapped the blanket and handed him a dog. It was a little thing, with soft creamy fur, who looked like he was very content to lay on Katie's lap. He tucked the dog into one arm, then offered her a hand. With muscles that seemed either sore or frozen— or both — she stepped out onto the space he had shoveled.

"We are headed down this way to an ice rink I used to skate at. I'll have to shovel the snow as we go, and you'll need to follow behind me holding the dog." He raised an eyebrow, asking if it was something she thought she could do in her current state.

"I've got this," she said.

He nodded. "Of course you do." He handed her the dog and then helped to get her blanket situated around herself and the dog, clutching it tight at the front. Then the two of them started making their way toward the rink. They walked with their heads down, trying to keep the falling snow off their faces.

It was cold and he was exhausted, but he had to admit that the landscape was pretty incredible. White blanketed everything, leaving only mounds indicating that a rock, or a shrub, or a mailbox was present. Even the sky was white. The kind of bluish-white that could only happen in the middle of the night during a snowstorm.

The most striking thing, though, was the silence. With no cars, no people, and just the steady fall of snow that seemed to mute every sound, the silence was a profound, enveloping quiet. As destructive as the snow was, it also brought with it a calm sort of peace.

"Connor," Katie said, her voice almost a wheeze. "Can we stop and rest? I'm just so cold, and my feet hurt so much, and I am so tired."

They were maybe twenty feet from the corner. Then they needed to cross a street, then cross the ice rink's parking lot to the front door. They were so close. They couldn't stop now— he needed to get her warm. He shook his head. "That's a really bad idea, especially with as cold as you are." He leaned the shovel's handle against the trunk of a tree, then scooped Katie up in his arms. The little dog yelped in surprise but then burrowed into the blanket at Katie's stomach.

"Are you good?"

She nodded, so he trudged his way through the snow, counting each step as he went to help him stay focused. He counted to the end of the sidewalk. Then he counted as they crossed the road. Then he counted to the front doors of the building. A small awning kept most of the snow away from the space nearest the doors, so he set

Katie down there and headed alongside the building to retrieve the key.

As he was walking back to the door, it was evident in the hunched way Katie stood that the cold had drained her of all her energy. She probably hadn't been able to sleep at all. And Katie wasn't someone who would just sit and wait for help— he could only guess how much energy she had expended trying to free her car. She looked ready to collapse at any moment.

Once inside, he helped Katie as they went around the rink to the backside. Knox was right— his office was unlocked. He, Katie, and the dog went inside, and he shut the door behind them to help hold in the heat. Then he found the space heater and turned it on. Katie whimpered in relief as the warm air started coming out.

"We need to get you into dry clothes." He had her sit in Knox's office chair while he pulled off her wet boots and equally wet socks. Then he pulled the pajama pants and socks out of his coat and said, "Change into these." He smiled at her. "They come pre-warmed. I'll turn around."

He turned his back to her until she said she was finished. Then he took off her coat, put it on the back of the office chair, then slipped out of his coat and helped her into it. His wasn't exactly dry on the outside, but it was dry on the inside, and the sleeves were much drier than hers.

"But what about you?"

"You do remember that I hang out on ice for a living?" When she gave a weak laugh, he said, "Don't worry about me."

He went to the corner of the office where Knox had a half-empty case of bottled water and grabbed a couple. He handed one to Katie. "Drink. Dehydration can lead to hypothermia much more quickly."

She guzzled the water, so maybe she had already been well on her way to hypothermia. Then she looked down at the floor for a moment before deciding to just lay down on it. He looked in the little closet in a corner and found a zippered hoodie. He rolled it up until it was roughly pillow-shaped and placed it under Katie's head, then spread the blanket over her.

He got the dog some water and got him settled just above Katie's head, snuggled into the dry part of her coat. He pulled out his phone and texted Emmalee to let her know that he found Katie and that they were sheltering at the ice rink. Then he lay down on the floor next to Katie. They were both lying on their sides, facing each other, him using one arm as a pillow.

He reached out and brushed Katie's hair away from her face, saying, "You're okay" and "We're going to be okay" until she fell asleep.

nineteen

KATIE

WHEN KATIE WOKE UP, all she knew was that she was gloriously warm and that her hip hurt. It took a minute of blinking at her surroundings to remember that she was on the floor in the office at the ice rink. She vaguely remembered Connor lying on the floor beside her as she fell asleep, but he wasn't there now.

She thought of Biscuit and found him curled up in her coat near her head. He looked so blissfully asleep. She gave him a little pet on the head, then stood up and stretched. Then she laughed when she saw the pajama pants she was wearing. She did remember changing into them last night, but she hadn't noticed that the fabric print was of pink flamingos, dressed in hockey gear, playing a fierce game of hockey.

It was so unbelievably sweet of Connor to brave such

a bad snowstorm to find her. She wasn't even sure *how* he found her. Or how he got them into this place. She spotted her cell phone that had been in her coat pocket — it was plugged into a charger on the desk of whoever's office this was.

She unplugged it and scrolled through her notifications. There were several texts from Emmalee, starting from when her phone had shut down during their conversation, asking if she was okay. They got increasingly panicked until the last one.

> Emmalee: I called Connor. Don't worry. He's got you.

Don't worry. He's got you.

Things got so much worse than she ever could've guessed they would. But he showed up when she needed him most. Just like when he showed up to help with the flowers. He was there when it mattered, even when she told him not to be. He somehow seemed to understand when she genuinely didn't want help with something and when she truly did need help but either didn't want to ask for help or really didn't want to accept it. She just kept finding new things about him to fall in love with.

She sent Emmalee a text thanking her for being such a great friend, and then she slid the phone into the pajama pants' pocket. She ran her hands over her face to help her wake up, then drained the rest of the water bottle that Connor had given her last night.

Then a thought occurred to her, and it felt ridiculous that it hadn't occurred to her sooner. Connor didn't say that he was leaving Denver, just that he was thinking about asking. It wasn't a done deal. She could fight for him; let him know how she really felt, because it mattered to her. He mattered to her. If he was going to leave, he wasn't going to leave not knowing how she felt.

She finger-combed her hair, then headed out of the office wearing Connor's socks and no shoes, in search of him. This was a small-town rink, so there weren't many places he could be. Sounds led her to the ice, and she found him skating in big lazy circles on the ice, looking at the ice like he was deep in thought.

He hadn't noticed her yet, so she just watched him. Hockey may be a hard-fought sport played by big, strong athletes, but this man was nothing but graceful on the ice. Every movement flowed. Even with the meandering nature of his turns, everything looked perfectly controlled. Effortless.

It was clear the moment he noticed her because he was suddenly alert, upright, focused. "You're awake already." He skated over to her with just a few strides and skidded to a stop right at the waist-high wall that separated the aisle where she stood and the ice, his skates spraying a small arc of ice. "It's still early."

She shrugged. "Probably because it's Christmas morning. It's the day you're supposed to wake up the earliest, right?"

He chuckled, but his eyes were searching hers, checking to see if she was okay.

"Or maybe it was because I could sense in my sleep that I was wearing awesome pajamas." She took a step back and motioned at the flamingos in all their glory. Then she met his eyes. "And the fact that I was so toasty warm. *Thank you.*"

He gave her a smile. "I'm just glad you're okay." He moved his hand, like he wanted to reach up and maybe cup her cheek but then decided against it.

"I need to apologize."

"No, I do."

She held up a hand. "Hold on. I really need to. I could tell last night that it was probably a bad idea to head out into the storm and that I was just being stubborn about it and not listening to reason. I was on edge from finding out that you wanted to leave and apparently decided to react by making a phenomenally bad decision. I'm very sorry that I made a choice that caused you to get into a bad situation to save me. And I'm also very grateful that you did."

"I don't want to be traded."

She froze. "You... don't?"

He shook his head. "No. I mean I did the day I was

traded here. But then I met you and everything changed."

"It did?"

He met her eyes. "Everything." And then, after a long moment, he put his hands on his hips and looked up, his feet skating him in a small, tight circle. "And then, after getting home from a hard game in Charlotte, I ran into my dad yesterday morning."

Her eyebrows shot up. "Oh?" She didn't know where his dad lived, but she had gotten the impression that it wasn't close.

He nodded. "We didn't talk for long. Just enough for me to notice that he had a new wife, a son, and a daughter, and to make a comment about him replacing us."

Katie winced.

"Yeah, I didn't handle it well. And then, apparently, because I'm a glutton for punishment, when I arrived in Mountain Springs yesterday, I drove past the house we used to live in."

"You mean the place where you lived when your parents' marriage imploded— "

"— and I became an angry teen. Yeah, that one. It was stupid, I know. It was like everything in a twenty-four-hour period started taking me down. First, smaller things, then bigger and bigger, and I decided to finish it off with a bang. To fully bury myself in every hard thing."

"Connor, that sounds awful. Why didn't you tell me? I could've helped." She paused for a moment. "Okay, I recognize the contradiction in wanting you to come to me for help when I didn't go to you for help. But I would have listened."

"You are really good at that. And at helping me to see the bigger picture." He tried to hide a smile and added, "As long as I don't lead with 'I want to be traded away from here.'"

She looked down, laughing quietly. "Yeah, probably best not to lead with that."

"Anyway, it kind of all got into my head and I started only looking at that, which wasn't so helpful. If I had looked at the whole picture, I'd have known exactly what I wanted. I want you."

A warmth and light filled her whole chest at hearing his words. "You know," she said, "I was fully ready to come out here and do everything I could to convince you to stay. Even with hair that has spent way too much time in a hood and while wearing hockey-playing flamingo pants."

"You definitely convinced me to stay." He reached out and placed a hand at the side of her neck, his thumb lightly brushing the skin just in front of her ear, and she leaned into his touch.

Then he wrapped his other arm around her waist, pulling her close, and gently pressed his lips against hers. There was something about this kiss that was different from any other they'd shared, and it wasn't just the waist-high wall that was between them. It felt more sure. More confident. She wrapped her arms around his neck and sunk into him, soaking in the feel of being cherished by this man that she couldn't imagine loving more, yet knowing that every day, she would love him more than she had the day before.

Eventually, they ended the kiss, and she looked out over the ice. "So... Do you think they have skates here that are my size?"

His eyebrows rose. "Do you skate?"

She shrugged. "Kind of. I haven't for years, but I went with friends for fun when I was a kid. I never had a teacher or a coach or anything. But I'd like to try."

He took her to the skate rental area and she put on a pair, walking over to the ice with wobbly ankles. With one hand on the short wall, she stepped onto the ice, and one skate slid more than the other. She had to hurry to try to pull her feet together. She went a little way on the ice, moving slowly and with tiny strides. Still holding onto the wall, Connor at her side.

"Are you good?"

She nodded. "I've got this."

"Of course you do."

She tried to let go of the wall but nearly fell. "No, no, I don't have this!"

In a second, Connor's strong arm was around her waist, supporting her. Her ankles were still feeling wobbly, but she dared let go of the wall, trusting in Connor's strength and balance. He skated around the rink with her, as slowly as she needed while she worked to find her balance and figure out how to move her legs. The further they went, the more she figured it out, and the more Connor loosened his arm, turning control over to her.

During their second time around the rink, she was doing so much better that he dropped his arm from her back and slipped his hand into hers. She grinned at him as she found that she could do it. She could stay upright and skate forward with only his hand as a failsafe.

The third time around, she was so proud of how well she was doing. It hit her that relationships were about helping each other. Supporting each other. Not feeling like she needed to be so independent that she pushed him away. It was about finding that beautiful interdependence where they helped and supported each other as they both fully became who they were supposed to be. She hadn't really understood the concept until now.

By the fourth time around, she had gotten to where she could skate a bit faster. As they went down the long straight part, she tipped her face up, feeling the wind from their speed blowing across her. She closed her eyes for a moment, knowing that he had her hand and would keep her going in the right direction. She felt free. Like a bird flying down low to a lake, skimming just above its surface.

As they reached the curved part of the rink at the end, Connor grabbed her other hand and spun the two of them in a circle before coming to a stop. She laughed at the joy of it. "I can see why you love this."

He grinned at her. "It's pretty great, isn't it?"

She grinned right back.

"Are you hungry?"

"Why? Are we going to walk to the nearest restaurant, find a hidden key, and go inside? Are there hidden keys everywhere? Do you know where they all are?"

Connor laughed an unrestrained laugh that she loved. "No, but Knox, the man who owns the rink, called a bit ago to see if we made it safely and to make sure that we are doing well. He said he keeps snacks in his office and told me where. Do you want breakfast?"

"I sure do," she said, realizing how hungry she was.

As they took off their skates and headed back to the office, he said, "Oh, and I texted your parents to let them know where we are."

Her eyes widened. "Thank you! I didn't even think of that— they're probably waking up about now."

In the office, Connor gathered protein bars, snack-sized bags of crackers and chips, and a couple of little cups of mandarin oranges. Biscuit woke up at hearing them, so Katie bent down and gave him a good rub on the sides of his cute face. She turned to Connor. "Do you think it's still snowing?"

"It stopped a bit ago." He put the snacks into the middle of her blanket, added three water bottles, then gathered the edges of the blanket up and put it over his shoulder. "Come with me."

Katie scooped up Biscuit, and then she walked with Connor along the aisle that separated the ice from the bleachers, and around to the front doors, which were in the middle of an area that made a big half circle with floor-to-ceiling windows.

The view beyond the glass was incredible. Deep snow covered everything, making it a sea of white. The sun was getting close to rising, and the sky was turning a beautiful pink that reflected on the snow below. "Have you ever seen anything so beautiful?" she asked.

She felt his eyes on her as he said, "Yes, I have."

Connor spread out the blanket, and the two of them sat down on it and ate a Christmas breakfast that wasn't exactly the traditional cinnamon rolls that her mom made, but it was now her favorite Christmas breakfast. They ate and played with Biscuit and chatted as the sky changed from pink to a light blue.

The moment the sun poked its head over the mountain, it lit up the snow, making it shine like it was made of silvery-golden glitter. She wasn't sure she'd seen anything so incredible.

"Katie?"

She looked over at him.

"Merry Christmas," he said and kissed her on the cheek.

twenty

CONNOR

CONNOR AND KATIE stayed in front of the big windows for a long time, just chatting and hanging out with Biscuit. The lack of sleep during the night was catching up with him, so Katie was sitting on the blanket, and he was lying with his head in her lap as she played with his hair. It was the most relaxed he'd been for as long as he could remember.

"Wouldn't a little Glacier's jersey look so cute on him?" Katie asked.

He chuckled. "It would." Biscuit yipped in a way that he was pretty sure meant that he agreed.

He thought about what his plan had been for Christmas before he got traded. It was so different from how he was spending Christmas morning, but he wouldn't have exchanged this morning for anything.

Katie's phone rang, and she answered it on speaker-phone. It was her mom. "Merry Christmas! Are you two doing okay?"

Katie looked at him and smiled. "We are. We're staying warm and everything."

"Oh, I'm so glad to hear that. What a scary night you had. You're at the ice rink, right?"

"Yep."

"Okay, well I've got some news— Noelle's water broke and she went into labor!"

"Really?" Katie grinned at Connor, happiness all over her face.

"They managed to track down someone with a Mini Ripsaw and a sled to take them to the hospital." She chuckled. "Jack was a little freaked out that he might have to deliver the baby himself."

He heard Katie's dad say in the background, "I don't blame him!"

"Anyway, her labor is progressing well, and they are guessing that she'll have the baby soon. They're sending the Mini Ripsaw around to get everyone, and it should be to you before long."

They immediately stood and started gathering everything into the blanket. After they hung up, Katie turned to him, practically bouncing in excitement. "Noelle's about to have her baby!" Biscuit seemed just as excited, so he was barking and turning around in circles.

Connor had put their boots, socks, and Katie's pants in front of the heater last night, so they were mostly dry. He'd put her coat in front of it, too, once Biscuit was no longer using it as a bed. Sadly, Katie changed from the pajama pants back into her jeans. With her wearing them, he'd decided that they were, indeed, his favorite pajamas.

Once they were all ready to go, it didn't take long before the guy driving the Mini Ripsaw showed up. It was basically an ATV that had tracks like a tank instead of wheels, and it was pulling a sled with seats that could easily fit four people. He locked up the rink, returned the key to its hiding spot, shook the driver's hand, and then climbed into the sled with Katie and Biscuit.

The vehicle seemed to have no problem at all traveling on top of the snow. "Has this been a busy morning for you?" he asked the driver.

"Oh, yeah," he said, grinning. "All night long. I live for storms like these."

The route to the hospital took them down the same path they had taken last night. The snow shovel he'd left by the tree was still there, but it was so covered in snow that it was almost unrecognizable as a shovel. When they went past the cross street where his car was, he looked in its direction, and even though he'd seen how much snow had fallen everywhere, he was surprised at how buried his car was.

Then they spotted Katie's car ahead, and she gasped and grabbed his arm. It was so covered in snow that its color almost couldn't be seen. "I can't believe I had just planned to wait out the storm." Her eyes were wide as she took it in. "Look at how much is on top! And on the sides! I probably couldn't even get my doors open right now." She brought her gloved hands up to cover her mouth as they drove past it, just staring at it.

Then she turned to him. "Did you see how much snow was in front of the exhaust? I would've had to get out so many times to clear it! And I would've gotten wetter each time. And that's only if the gas I had in my tank would've lasted through the night."

He wrapped an arm around her, pulling her close. "I'm so glad that Emmalee told me you were stuck." It made him sick to imagine her being in there all night long.

She turned her head to meet his eyes. "Thank you again for coming to save me after I made a really stupid choice."

He smiled. "And thank you for saving me from almost making a really stupid choice."

"What do you say we keep saving each other?"

"Deal," he said. "And what do you say to always asking each other for help, too?"

"Deal."

They were about a block past Katie's car when there

started being houses again, and they heard some kids calling out, "Glacier! Glacier!" He wasn't sure why, but as they neared, Biscuit's ears twitched and he stood on Katie's lap, then started barking.

"Oh!" Katie said. "Are those your owners?"

When they reached the kids and their dad, who were all outside in snow gear, looking for their dog and calling out "Glacier!" she held up the little dog. "Is this him?"

"Glacier!" the kids shouted. The dad tromped through the snow that was well past his knees over to them. The little dog looked like he wanted to run to them but was afraid to jump into the snow. Good. Because if the little guy did, he'd probably sink and be completely buried.

Katie handed off the dog to the dad, and he said, "I cannot thank you enough for bringing him to us. I was really worried we wouldn't ever find him."

As the dad took the dog over to the kids, Katie said, "Look how happy they are!"

He gave her a squeeze and kissed her hair as the kids shouted, "Thank you!"

She turned to him. "He was a pretty cool dog, wasn't he."

"He was." This morning had made him imagine more than once the two of them sharing a life together and having a dog just like Biscuit. And kids. He really wanted to have kids. They thanked the driver when he dropped them off at the hospital before he left to go help other people in the snow.

When they got inside, Mr. Allred met them and walked them to the labor and delivery wing. "She had the baby not too long ago," Mr. Allred said. "Elizabeth is in there with them right now. They're about to move her to her room, and after seeing the crowd of us, they said they'd get her the biggest one they could. We should be able to see them and the new baby soon after that."

At labor and delivery, they found Katie's entire family, along with Rachel, Nick, Aiden, and Holly. They all hugged Katie and Connor and said, "Merry Christmas!" and they all shared with each other their stories about Christmas morning and the crazy snowstorm. Everyone treated him just like they did every other member of the family. This big family had all welcomed him with open arms from the very start. He'd never felt a part of another family so quickly before.

It hit him that maybe he didn't need to feel so bad that he was far from family. He had family here now, too.

Elizabeth came into the waiting room and said, "Okay, she's in her own room and ready for you now. You won't be able to hold the baby or get too close, but you can come in and see."

They followed her down the hall and filed into Noelle's room. Noelle was lying in the bed, the swaddled baby in her arms, and Jack was seated in the chair right next to Noelle, the baby's little fingers wrapped around one of his. Both parents looked tired but were beaming.

Everyone talked over one another as they told Jack and Noelle how beautiful their baby was, and he really was. Seeing their little family just made Connor yearn for the same. Katie looked up at him and smiled in a way that told him that maybe she was thinking the same thing.

"What are you going to name him?" Holly asked.

"Since it's Christmas," Nick said, "I vote for Nick."

"I think you should name him Dasher," Aiden said. "There's a kid in our class named Dasher."

"You can name a kid Dasher," Katie's brother-in-law, Corbin said, "but I'm not sure you can name a kid who was born on Christmas Day 'Dasher,' or people will only think of the reindeer playing games."

"How about Joseph?" Julianne offered.

"You can't name him Jesus's dad's name," Holly said, "he's *the baby*!"

Then everyone started giving their helpful suggestions.

"How about Cole?"

"Like what you get in your stocking if you're naughty?"

"Oh, Douglas! Because Douglas Firs are Christmas trees."

"Name him Winter because he was born in a snowstorm!"

"*Winter Meadows*? That's kind of a weird mental image."

"No, it's not. Meadows get snowed on, too."

Noelle, who was gazing down at her baby, said, "We've decided to name him Gabriel."

Katie looked up at Connor and smiled, and he pulled her into a hug. "Isn't he the sweetest?"

"He really is."

Katie turned back to look at the baby and her hands fluttered like she was having a hard time not going over to Noelle. "Oh, I can't wait until I can hold him!"

And he couldn't wait until she could hold one of their own.

KATIE

One Year Later

"The rehearsal went pretty well, don't you think?" Connor asked Katie as they walked into the room with the tables all set for the rehearsal dinner.

"If you consider how many kids are part of the wedding party," Katie said, "I think it went *very* well." Family had been a big part of their wedding plans, and she was glad that it was as important to Connor as it was to her.

Her nieces and nephews were going to be flower girls and ring bearers, or had tasks of greeting guests, taking gifts to the gift table, handing out wedding favors, and being junior bridesmaids and groomsmen. Aiden and Holly had been calling Katie's parents "grandma" and "grandpa" for the last couple of years, and somewhere along the way, they had just become part of the family. Katie considered them her niece and nephew every bit as much as she did her actual nieces and nephews, so they had assignments at the wedding, too.

Besides Emmalee, Katie's bridesmaids included her four sisters and Connor's recently engaged sister, Laura, whom Katie had become good friends with over the past year, despite living in a different state from her. Connor's groomsmen were Katie's four brothers-in-law, his best friend, Erik, a few of his other teammates, and Vaughan — his team captain from the Thunderstorm.

The Thunderstorm played the Glaciers in Denver last night, followed by two days without a game for both teams. With as perfectly as that lined up, they couldn't pass up the opportunity to plan their wedding for tomorrow so that his old teammates could be present, too. The fact that the date was almost a year to the day since Connor ran into her at that department store the night before they first met officially was a happy bonus.

Tonight, with all their closest family and friends surrounding them, they were going to have a much more casual dinner before they got married tomorrow. And Connor's dad was even present!

She'd been so proud of Connor for reaching out to him. There had never been abuse in his family, and before things between his parents got bad and his dad just disappeared, the two of them had been quite close. Connor seemed to feel that it was a relationship he really wanted in his life, so she supported him in moving forward at whatever pace he wanted to go. He and his dad weren't back to the same level of closeness they'd had when Connor was young— they still had a long way to go in repairing their relationship— but they had made enough progress that Connor really wanted him there.

As they made their way toward their seats at the tables in the room, Noelle and Jack came up to them, their one-year-old in Jack's arms. Noelle said, "Well, what do you think?" She spun in a circle, then struck a pose, showing off her dress that was a gorgeous deep blue.

"You picked out a good one," Connor said. "It looks beautiful on you."

Noelle grinned. "Thank you. For the compliment and for the dress."

"I'm sorry that it took me nearly eleven years to replace the one I ruined when Katie was wearing it at that dance."

"I'll forgive the delay— this one is definitely an upgrade. But I vote we keep this room a punch bowl-free zone for tonight."

Connor laughed and said, "Deal."

When Noelle, Jack, and little Gabriel turned to take their seats at the table, Katie turned to Connor, straightening his tie. "And what are you going to do to make up for my dance being ruined all those years ago?"

Connor leaned in closer to her, his breath tickling her ear. "I'm going to give you such an amazing time dancing at our wedding tomorrow that you will no longer even be able to remember another dance."

A smile spread across her face. "Oh, yeah?"

"Or we can start tonight if you'd rather. Out there on the patio, after the dinner."

Katie glanced toward the patio. "It's snowing."

Connor shrugged. "It's Christmastime and it was at a Christmas dance, so it feels appropriate."

"And I do remember a pretty amazing kiss in the snow."

"Maybe we can recreate that while we're at it."

Katie grinned. She felt tingly and breathless just knowing that tomorrow, she got to marry this man. "Come on," she said. "Let's get to our seats."

She loved that they got this more casual chance to enjoy the company of everyone they loved before the wedding tomorrow. And it gave all of those people plenty of opportunities to give them plenty of roasts.

"We joke about how speedy Connor is on the ice," Vaughan said. "We just hadn't expected him to go from meeting someone to marriage this quickly."

Connor sat up straight. "Was it fast? Because I was

ready to marry her back in April when I proposed. I didn't think this day would ever get here."

"It's a good thing you like things to go quickly," Katie's brother-in-law, Ben, said, "since you'll only get the three days over Christmas break for your honeymoon!"

"If you get to go at all." Laura held up her phone. "I saw that there's a big storm coming in that's going to shut down the airport."

Connor pointed at his sister. "Okay, that's not even funny. It's not true, right?"

By the look on Laura's face, it really wasn't. "Don't worry," Katie said. "We're taking a long, slow, luxurious honeymoon in the off-season."

"And we're going to enjoy every minute of it," Connor said, then lifted her hand and placed a kiss on the back of it.

"A year ago," Noelle said, "everyone our age in Mountain Springs knew Connor as the guy who started a fight at a school dance, making us lose our dance privileges. Some in town knew him as the kid who used to play hockey at Mountain Springs' rink. Others knew him as the kid who moved away and then became an NHL star."

Aiden piped up, "And everyone at my school knew him as the elf who tore his pants!" and they all laughed.

"As great as those memories are," Noelle said, "I'm

glad everyone in this area now knows the real Connor. And I'm especially glad that we get to." She held up her glass. "Welcome to the family, Connor."

Katie loved the smile that overtook Connor's face. He gave her hand a squeeze and held up his own glass.

The Christmas outreach program had gone so well for so many of the players that quite a few continued going to the same areas they'd been assigned at Christmastime throughout the year. Connor did the same, helping out with lots of town projects and celebrations. He was around enough, helping, that everyone in the Mountain Springs, Nestled Hollow, and Copper Mountains area knew him well. Half of them would be coming to the wedding tomorrow.

The rest of her sisters got in on the roasts, too. Becca did a whole bit about Katie's "I do it!" tendencies that got the group roaring with laughter. "Luckily," she said, "we talked her out of being the videographer for her own wedding. Seriously, though, Katie has come a long way since meeting Connor. Now she saves 'I do it' for things like beating everyone at board games, challenging Connor to ice skating races, and arguing with GPS directions."

Katie laughed. The part about her wanting to be her own videographer was an exaggeration. She wanted *her company* to do it. Or, more specifically, the assistant she now had. Her business had exploded over the past year.

Enough that she was no longer worried about living in her car and eating cold Ramen. The Glaciers had loved her work and had since asked her to do several other projects for them. And with how much they had shown her footage of Connor in ads, she was getting clients left and right, both in the Mountain Springs area and in Denver and its surrounding cities.

"Katie might have gotten past a lot of her need to do everything herself," Emmalee said, "but I think she gave some of it to Connor."

"Not just to Connor," Bradshaw said, pointing between him, Connor, Erik, Davis, and Calloway. "We *all* wanted to make the centerpieces."

And then all five men high-fived each other and nodded and talked about how they were basically professional florists now and how much everyone was going to love their centerpieces tomorrow. Katie loved that they were all not just willing but excited to do it again. They even thanked Emmalee several times for letting them. Of course, it put Emmalee on a high that she still hadn't come down from.

Plus, Katie was pretty sure that Emmalee had a crush on Bradshaw. And after covering for her florist friend with the last-minute wedding a year ago, especially since the centerpieces and bridesmaid bouquets were made by NHL players, Emmalee's business had exploded, too. Katie was no longer working for her friend, but

Emmalee had been able to hire two assistants in her place.

Erik said, "I know you'd never guess it by looking at Connor now, as he wears his Denver colors with pride, but there was a time when he actually wanted to leave this great state."

Several people gasped in mock shock.

"Seriously, though, you two. Congrats on buying your new place. I hope you have many happy memories there."

Katie looked at Connor, and he had an expression of serene happiness on his face. His eyes were lit up just like they always were when something made him excited. She was excited, too. They just closed on the place, and she couldn't wait to start living there with him. It was so cute and so exactly their style. It was halfway between the arena and Mountain Springs, so it would be easy for her to meet with clients in either location, and Connor wouldn't have to go far to go to practices or a game.

They knew that Connor could get traded at any time to any team in the U.S. or Canada. If that happened, they would go wherever the NHL took them. It'd be an adventure. And if they did move away, they hoped that eventually, they would find their way back to Mountain Springs and raise a family there.

Katie's dad stood and said, "You know, from the

moment these two met, we could tell there was something special between them. And it wasn't just because their last names were Allred and Greene and it was Christmastime."

It wasn't the first time they'd heard the "all red and green" comments. They decided to embrace it. In fact, the sign at the door to their wedding ceremony was a play on ones they'd seen before. It read, *Just like Christmas colors, Allreds and Greenes belong side by side. So pick a seat anywhere— you're loved by the groom and the bride.* It might be a little cheesy, but Katie loved it.

"And since they fell in love at Christmastime," her dad continued, "getting married right now feels perfect."

She smiled and thought back to a year ago when they were on the hay ride and Aiden asked Connor if he was already in love, and Holly suggested that maybe Connor could fall in love on the hay ride. She'd heard the two kids telling people that they had, indeed, fallen in love on that night. They may have been right.

"I wish you two all the best life has to offer," her dad said. "You already have each other, and that's all you really need." Then he held his glass high, and everyone else did, as well.

She and Connor looked at each other, smiling. Then she leaned against him, laying her head against his shoulder, and he kissed her hair. Tomorrow, she was going to put on a beautiful dress, walk down that aisle, and say "I do" to the man she'd been falling more in love with every single day over the past year. If she got to spend her life with him, that really was all she needed.

At the end of dinner, as everyone was getting into their cars and heading home or to a hotel for the night, she and Connor shared a moment together just outside the building as light snow fell softly from the sky.

He brushed a snowflake from her forehead, just above her eyebrow. His fingertips were soft and gentle, like always. His face was full of so much love, anticipation, and hope for their future together. She felt the same buzzing in both her heart and mind.

"Tomorrow," she breathed.

"Tomorrow. I feel like I've been waiting my entire life for this moment."

"You're not getting cold feet?"

He chuckled. "You do remember that I hang out on ice for a living? I'm impervious to cold feet. You?"

"They've never been hotter."

"Katie," Emmalee called from where she stood at the open driver's door of her car, "come on. We've got to get home so you can get beauty sleep before the big day!"

Connor's eyes shifted for a moment toward Emmalee, and then his eyes returned to hers with a longing that had become very familiar. "Tonight's the last time that 'going home' means going to separate places."

Tomorrow night, they'd be leaving to go to *their* home. Hers and Connor's. Heading home had never sounded so wonderful. A smile overtook her face. "I can't wait. See you tomorrow, my soon-to-be husband."

Connor's smile was every bit as big as hers. "Tomorrow, my soon-to-be wife."

Five Years Later

Noelle

Jack put the car into park after pulling into the driveway at Noelle's parents' house, and then they all started getting out of the car. Gabriel, her son who was turning six tomorrow, started running up the curved sidewalk toward the door.

"Gabe, honey," she called out, "will you come back and help your sister so she doesn't slip on the snow?"

Her four-year-old daughter, Evalena, had just gotten out of the car, put her hands on her hips, and said, "No, I can do it by myself," just as Gabriel said, "It's not slippery."

"Can you help carry in the presents then?" Jack asked, which were apparently the magic words, because Gabe was back in a flash to help, begging his dad to load them up high on his arms.

Noelle opened the back door and helped her one-year-old, Leo, out of his car seat and into her arms. He was the sweetest little boy with the softest curls. She gave him a kiss on the cheek as Jack got their dish of freshly roasted cinnamon butternut squash out of the trunk. He came over to her, wrapped his arm around her shoulders, and placed a kiss on her temple. "Happy birthday, sweetheart."

She smiled and gave him a kiss right on the lips. Christmas Eve— her birthday— got busier with the birth of each of their three kids, but Jack never ceased to make her feel like she was worth the sun, the moon, and the stars every time.

Actually, he never ceased to make her feel like that every day, not just on her birthday.

As they went around the car and to the sidewalk, Evalena was still standing in the same spot, just gazing at all the decorations that covered the front lawn. She looked up at them with her big eyes and said, "They're just so beautiful! Don't they make you want to cry because they're so pretty?"

Noelle loved that Evalena thought so. All of her kids loved Christmas. She made sure they were all growing up enjoying the same traditions that Noelle had loved doing with her gran-gran. And she made sure they knew all about the woman she'd loved so fiercely so she wouldn't ever be forgotten.

"They are beautiful," Jack said, and he leaned down to hold her hand with the hand that wasn't holding the baking dish and walked with her up to the front door.

Noelle followed behind with Leo, taking in how adorable it was to see her husband holding her little girl's hand. She would never tire of seeing that. Or of seeing him care for and play with any of their kids. She had known Jack would be a great dad by seeing the way he interacted with his nephew, Aiden, when they were first dating, but it had grabbed hold of her heart like nothing else to see him with their own kids.

They went inside and greeted and hugged her parents, Becca and her family, and Hope and her family, and then she got Leo settled and playing with some blocks that her parents had placed near the Christmas tree.

When the front door opened, she leaned forward to see around the wall toward to see Nick and Rachel come in with Aiden and Holly. Holly must've had a hockey game or practice because she was wearing her team's jersey, looking pretty proud of herself. Aiden walked beside her, holding a present in his hands.

She couldn't believe how tall the two of them had

grown! They were both thirteen, so she guessed it was to be expected, but they had just shot up in the past little while. Aiden might have passed her height, even.

She got up off the floor to greet Jack's sister and her husband. Then Jack put an arm around Noelle, gave her a squeeze and a kiss to the temple, and said, "I'm going to help out in the kitchen. Have a seat on the couch and socialize. You've had a long day and it's your birthday— kick your feet up."

"You're the best, you know that?"

Jack gave her that smile she loved so much. "I try to be."

Rachel

In the festive home where Rachel and her family now spent every Christmas Eve, she hugged all her brother's in-laws who had become her family as well. She loved this place and she loved these people.

Nick went up to their nephew, Gabriel, and, crouched down, said, "How's my favorite six-year-old?"

"Great!" Gabe said. "Because not only is it my mom's birthday, but Santa is coming tonight, and I really hope — and I mean crossing-all-my-fingers hoping— that he brings me this Lego set I'm really wanting. And not only that, but tomorrow is *my* birthday! This really is the greatest time of the whole entire year."

"It sure is," Nick said. Then he turned and chatted with their niece, Evalena, his "favorite four-year-old," and then he told Leo that he was as cute as ever.

Gosh, she loved this man. She loved seeing how great he was with kids, especially with her brother's kids, and she loved seeing him with their own kids. Even now, as Aiden and Holly were entering their teenage years, he was still great with them. Even when they really tried to test exactly how much patience he had. So far, Aiden and Holly had learned two things— that they still hadn't seen the limits of their dad's patience, and that he loved them unconditionally.

As soon as Julianne and her family came in the house, their ten-year-old, Tommy, called out "Happy birthday to Noelle," and everyone else replied with "And to Noelle a good night!"

Aiden, present in hand, sat down on the couch next to Noelle. He might be an official teenager now and had been growing like crazy lately, but he still never lost the way he sat down with a bounce anytime he took a seat on the couch. He handed the gift to Noelle and said, "I made you a birthday present."

"You have a present for me? Aww! And you made it?"

Aiden's smile was wide as his Aunt Noelle opened the package. It was a ten-inch square piece of art that was maybe two inches thick and made of resin. He had poured the resin in layers, carving parts of the intricate lines of a snowflake into each layer with a little tool before adding the next layer. Each of the layers was a slightly different shade of blue or silver, and the end result was a beautiful masterpiece. The artist that her little boy had turned into never ceased to amaze her.

Noelle was pretty amazed, too, and so touched. It warmed her momma heart to watch their interaction. Nick came up behind her and wrapped his arms around her shoulders, hugging her. She reached up to place her arm on his and leaned her head into his arm.

Then her eyes caught her daughter in the kitchen as she went up to Connor. Connor had been cutting Brussels sprouts but stopped when she neared and came around the counter to talk to her. "Did you win?"

"Still undefeated!" Holly said with a grin on her face that hadn't left since the game yesterday.

Connor put out his palms and she slapped them with hers, then put out her palms and he did the same, and then they bumped fists. "Right on! Did you score?"

Holly folded her arms, looking pretty satisfied. "Twice."

"We've got some pretty great kids, don't we?" Nick said, his breath warming her ear.

"We do," Rachel said. "And a pretty great life."

Nick had been able to continue working four days a

week at home, only going into the office one day a week, for their entire marriage. It had allowed her to do really well at her job, knowing that he was able to take care of things on the home front as needed.

Plus, she had passed the five-year mark of being cancer-free over a year ago. Which meant that she no longer had to have that deep down, constant worry that it could come back. She hadn't realized how big a part of her had been worrying without her even realizing she was doing it until that threat was gone and she experienced the freedom of living without it.

She looked around at everything. At this big, beautiful family. At Aiden and Holly. At her husband, Nick. All of them together, celebrating Christmas. All of this wasn't anything she was sure she would *ever* get. It made having it all the sweeter, and she would never stop being grateful for every single bit of her incredible life.

She turned so she was facing Nick and wrapped her arms around him. She gave him a kiss on the lips, then said, "Thank you for being part of what makes my life so great."

Nick grinned, not entirely following her train of thought, but clearly enjoying it.

Katie

Katie and Connor had been trying to get pregnant from pretty close to the day they got married five years ago. In the beginning, it was fine that each month they found out that they weren't. The extra time they had with just the two of them gave them a chance to really bond as a couple and to figure out who they were separately, who they were together, and how to best support each other.

And it gave her time to figure out life being married to a hockey player who had 82 games a year, all while her company was growing at a rate fast enough that she was constantly having to figure it out anew.

But as the years went on, it became a lot harder. They both just really *really* wanted children. As much as she loved holding each of her new nieces and nephews, the emotions she experienced as she did were so much more complex and difficult when they wanted so badly to have their own.

And now they were. The fertility treatments they'd been doing for what felt like an eternity had finally worked. Not only had they worked, but they were going to be having twins. She was now thirteen weeks along, and things looked fantastic and the babies were so healthy. After their last doctor's visit, she and Connor decided that they were ready to share the news with everyone.

And because it was Christmas Eve and she was going to be showing the annual Allred Family Christmas Video that she made every year, they decided that they would make the announcement part of the video. She'd made a lot of these videos over the years, but none of them had been as fun— or made her tear up as much— as this one.

Since she filmed events for a living, she made sure to have the camera rolling at all the important parts of their lives. The video tonight had clips of them with their eyes glued to the pregnancy test that Katie held, waiting for the results, and the jumping up and down, cries of joy, and hugging when it revealed that the test was positive. The doctor's visit where they confirmed it. The looks of surprise, joy, and lots of shock during the ultrasound when they found out that two little babies were growing inside her.

Her stomach was getting all fluttery just thinking about pushing play on that video tonight and watching everyone's reactions to the news.

It had been a long, hard journey to get to this point. But after facing all the emotional, physical, and mental struggles of infertility together, she and Connor were so much stronger as a couple than they ever could've been without. Katie was sure they could face absolutely anything together, side by side. Connor could be traded to another team across the country, or even Canada, the day before she gave birth to her twins, and they could handle it.

She looked over at him from where they were cutting

up vegetables next to each other in her parents' kitchen. After making sure no one was close enough to hear, she said, "Please don't get traded to another team the day before I give birth."

He chuckled. "I won't."

She knew he wouldn't. Her due date was in the off-season, so if he did get traded, it wouldn't be rushed like it was when he was traded to the Glaciers. At least she expected the births to happen in the off-season. But the Glaciers could go to the playoffs, and she could have the twins early. Twins usually came early.

"But even if you did, we could handle it, right?"

He gave her a kiss. "Together, we can handle anything."

"Even twins."

He nodded. "Even twins. *Especially* twins." He cut a few more carrots, and then paused before adding, "Maybe even a move."

Katie's eyebrows rose. "A move?"

He lifted a shoulder. "What do you think? We've always talked about moving back here when we have kids. I don't think we should hold off just because I might get traded to another team someday. I might stay with the Glaciers until I retire from hockey. And it'll probably be easier to get the house before the babies come because then we can get it ready for them."

Katie let go of the knife and the cauliflower she'd

been cutting and turned to face Connor, putting her hands on his cheeks, and pulled him toward her, planting a kiss on his lips. She hadn't even realized that a happy tear had escaped her eye until she felt its wetness as it made its way down her cheek.

She pulled back just a bit but kept her hands on his face. "I think we're ready for all of it, Connor. The house, the babies, and whatever life throws at us."

"I think we are, too," he said and kissed her again.

Did you miss Noelle's and Jack's story in The Christmas Pact or Rachel's and Nick's in The Christmas Bet?

Get the books you are missing

Want to read more Christmas romances by Meg Easton?

Get *Stockings, Snow, and Mistletoe* —two full-length Christmas romances to snuggle up with and swoon over. Both are full of heart, humor, hope, and all the magic of Christmas wrapped up in one holiday-filled collection.

Meg Easton is the *USA Today* bestselling author of contemporary romances and romantic comedies with fun, memorable, swoon-worthy characters, and settings you'll want to pack up and move to. She lives at the foot of a mountain with her name on it (or at least one letter of her name) in Utah. She loves gardening, bike riding, baking, swimming before the sun rises, and spending time with her husband and three kids.

She can be found online at www.megeaston.com

Sign up to receive her newsletter and stay up to date with new releases, get exclusive bonus content, and more.

If you liked this book please leave a review. Your review can help other readers find books they might fall in love with.

youtube.com/@megeastonauthor
bookbub.com/authors/meg-easton
instagram.com/megeaston_author
facebook.com/MegEastonBooks
tiktok.com/@megeaston_author

www.ingramcontent.com/pod-product-compliance
Lightning Source LLC
Chambersburg PA
CBHW020750190726
48285CB00006B/1958